核心 素養 108課綱

# 讀出英語

# 核心素養 4

## 九大技巧打造閱讀力

作者● Owain Mckimm    譯者●劉嘉珮    審訂● Helen Yeh

跨領域主題 ╳ 生活化體裁 ╳ 250道閱讀題

精準貼合108 課綱　高效培養核心素養
用英語打造閱讀、分析、整合力！

MP3

寂天雲 APP

## 如何下載 MP3 音檔

❶ 寂天雲 APP 聆聽：掃描書上 QR Code 下載
「寂天雲－英日語學習隨身聽」APP。加入會員
後，用 APP 內建掃描器再次掃描書上 QR
Code，即可使用 APP 聆聽音檔。

❷ 官網下載音檔：請上「寂天閱讀網」
（www.icosmos.com.tw），註冊會員／登入後，
搜尋本書，進入本書頁面，點選「MP3 下載」
下載音檔，存於電腦等其他播放器聆聽使用。

# Contents

## Unit 1 | Reading Skills 閱讀技巧

| 體裁 / 主題 | 議題 | 素養 |
|---|---|---|
| **passage** 文章 + **bullet points** 列點<br>inspiration for teens 青少年啟發 | life<br>生命教育 | self-advancement<br>自我精進 |
| **website** 網站<br>life 生活 | reading literacy<br>閱讀素養教育 | information and technology literacy<br>科技資訊 |
| **news clip** 新聞短片<br>sport 體育 | outdoor education<br>戶外教育 | physical and mental wellness 身心素質 |
| **passage** 文章 + **bullet points** 列點<br>health & body 健康與身體 | career planning<br>生涯規劃教育 | physical and mental wellness 身心素質 |
| **poem** 詩<br>relationship 人際關係 | family education<br>家庭教育 | interpersonal relationship<br>人際關係 |
| **poster** 海報<br>school life 學校生活 | technology<br>科技教育 | planning and execution<br>規劃執行 |
| **passage** 文章 + **bullet points** 列點<br>relationship 人際關係 | morality<br>道德教育 | interpersonal relationship<br>人際關係 |
| **conversation** 對話<br>weather & climate 天氣與氣候 | environment<br>環境教育 | logical thinking<br>系統思考 |
| **passage** 文章<br>famous or interesting people 知名或有趣的人物 | information<br>資訊教育 | information and technology literacy<br>科技資訊 |
| **magazine article** 雜誌文章<br>science 科學 | reading literacy<br>閱讀素養教育 | problem solving<br>解決問題 |

## Unit 2　Word Study 字彙學習

| 體裁 / 主題 | 議題 | 素養 |
|---|---|---|
| **diary** 日記<br>interests and hobbies 興趣與嗜好 | reading literacy<br>閱讀素養教育 | self-advancement<br>自我精進 |
| **notice** 通知<br>safety 安全 | security<br>安全教育 | physical and mental wellness 身心素質 |
| **group chat** 多人聊天<br>relationship 人際關係 | morality<br>道德教育 | innovation and adaptation<br>創新應變 |
| **email** 電子郵件<br>life 生活 | reading literacy<br>閱讀素養教育 | problem solving<br>解決問題 |
| **passage** 文章<br>language & communication 語言與溝通 | multiculturalism<br>多元文化教育 | cultural understanding<br>多元文化 |
| **passage** 文章<br>animals 動物 | life<br>生命教育 | logical thinking<br>系統思考 |
| **card** 卡片<br>relationship 人際關係 | family education<br>家庭教育 | interpersonal relationship 人際關係 |
| **passage** 文章<br>science 科學 | reading literacy<br>閱讀素養教育 | logical thinking<br>系統思考 |
| **passage** 文章<br>inspiration for teens 青少年啟發 | career planning<br>生涯規劃教育 | self-advancement<br>自我精進 |
| **news clip** 新聞短片<br>environment 環境 | environment<br>環境教育 | citizenship<br>公民意識 |

| | | |
|---|---|---|
| **poster** 海報<br>health & body 健康與身體 | life<br>生命教育 | citizenship<br>公民意識 |
| **passage** 文章<br>culture 文化 | multiculturalism<br>多元文化教育 | cultural understanding<br>多元文化 |
| **passage** 文章<br>history 歷史 | international education<br>國際教育 | semiotics<br>符號運用 |
| **website** 網站<br>travel 旅遊 | outdoor education<br>戶外教育 | global understanding<br>國際理解 |

| 閱讀策略 | 文章 |
|---|---|

## Unit 3　Study Strategies 學習策略

| 體裁 / 主題 | 議題 | 素養 |
|---|---|---|
| **passage** 文章<br>animals 動物 | global ocean<br>海洋教育 | logical thinking<br>系統思考 |
| **passage** 文章<br>gender equality 性別平等 | gender equality<br>性別平等教育 | expression<br>溝通表達 |
| **poster** 海報<br>school life 學校生活 | reading literacy<br>閱讀素養教育 | self-advancement<br>自我精進 |
| **passage** 文章<br>health & body 健康與身體 | life 生命教育 | problem solving<br>解決問題 |
| **passage** 文章 + **bullet points** 列點<br>health & body 健康與身體 | reading literacy<br>閱讀素養教育 | physical and mental<br>wellness 身心素質 |
| **passage** 文章<br>career 職涯 | career planning<br>生涯規劃教育 | planning and<br>execution<br>規劃執行 |

| | | |
|---|---|---|
| **map** 地圖<br>environment 環境 | energy<br>能源教育 | innovation and<br>adaptation 創新應變 |
| **line chart** 折線圖<br>animals 動物 | reading literacy<br>閱讀素養教育 | moral praxis<br>道德實踐 |
| **bar chart** 長條圖<br>society 社會 | international<br>education 國際教育 | citizenship<br>公民意識 |
| **table** 表格<br>environment 環境 | environment<br>環境教育 | logical thinking<br>系統思考 |
| **pie chart** 圓餅圖<br>health & body 健康與身體 | life<br>生命教育 | physical and mental<br>wellness 身心素質 |
| **timeline** 時間軸<br>famous or interesting people<br>知名或有趣的人物 | international<br>education<br>國際教育 | global<br>understanding<br>國際理解 |
| **glossary** 術語表<br>psychology 心理學 | life<br>生命教育 | physical and<br>mental wellness<br>身心素質 |
| **table of contents** 目錄<br>inspiration for teens 青少年啟發 | career planning<br>生涯規劃教育 | logical thinking<br>系統思考 |

## Unit 4  Final Review 綜合練習

| 體裁 / 主題 | 議題 | 素養 |
|---|---|---|
| index 索引<br>plants 植物 | outdoor education<br>戶外教育 | planning and execution<br>規劃執行 |
| website search results<br>網站搜尋結果<br>life 生活 | information<br>資訊教育 | information and technology literacy<br>科技資訊 |
| | | |
| passage 文章<br>architecture 建築 | energy<br>能源教育 | innovation and adaptation 創新應變 |
| passage 文章<br>arts & literature 藝術與文學 | multiculturalism<br>多元文化教育 | artistic appreciation<br>藝術涵養 |
| passage 文章<br>psychology 心理學 | life<br>生命教育 | physical and mental wellness 身心素質 |
| passage 文章<br>plants 植物 | security<br>安全教育 | logical thinking<br>系統思考 |
| website 網站<br>school life 學校生活 | morality<br>道德教育 | expression<br>溝通表達 |
| instructions 操作指南<br>life 生活 | reading literacy<br>閱讀素養教育 | problem solving<br>解決問題 |
| passage 文章<br>inspiration for teens 青少年啟發 | morality<br>道德教育 | self-advancement<br>自我精進 |
| passage 文章 + bullet points 列點<br>culture 文化 | multiculturalism<br>多元文化教育 | cultural understanding<br>多元文化 |
| Venn diagram 文氏圖<br>animals 動物 | life 生命教育 | logical thinking<br>系統思考 |
| recipe 食譜<br>food & drinks 食物與飲料 | reading literacy<br>閱讀素養教育 | planning and execution 規劃執行 |

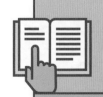

# Introduction

本套書共四冊，專為英語初學者設計，旨在**增進閱讀理解能力**並**提升閱讀技巧**。全套書符合 108 課綱要旨，強調**跨領域、生活化學習**，文章按照教育部公布的**九大核心素養**與 **19 項議題設計**撰寫，為讀者打造扎實的英語閱讀核心素養能力。

每冊內含 50 篇文章，主題包羅萬象，包括**文化、科學、自然、文學**等，內容以**日常生活常見體裁**寫成，舉凡**電子郵件、邀請函、廣告、公告、對話**皆收錄於書中，以多元主題及多變體裁，豐富讀者閱讀體驗，引導讀者從生活中學習，並將學習運用於生活。每篇文章之後設計**五道閱讀理解題**，依不同閱讀技巧重點精心撰寫，訓練統整、分析及應用所得資訊的能力，同時為日後的國中教育會考做準備。

# Key Features 本書特色

## 1. 按文章難度分級，可依程度選用適合的級數

全套書難度不同，方便各程度的學生使用，以文章字數、高級字詞使用數、文法難度、句子長度分為一至四冊，如下方表格所示：

| 文章字數<br>（每篇） | 國中 1200 字<br>（每篇） | 國中 1201 - 2000 字<br>（每篇） | 高中字彙<br>（3 - 5 級）<br>（每篇） | 文法 | 句子最長字數 |
|---|---|---|---|---|---|
| Book 1<br>120 - 150 | 93% | 7 字 | 3 字 | 國一 | 15 字 |
| Book 2<br>150 - 180 | 86% | 15 字 | 6 字 | 國二 | 18 字 |
| Book 3<br>180 - 210 | 82% | 30 字 | 7 字 | 國三 | 25 字 |
| Book 4<br>210 - 250 | 75% | 50 字 | 12 字 | 進階 | 28 字 |

## 2. 按文章難度分級，可依程度選用適合的級數

全書**主題多元**，有**青少年生活、家庭、商業、環境、健康、節慶、文化、動物、文學、旅遊**等，帶領讀者以英語探索知識、豐富生活，同時拉近學習與日常的距離。

## 3. 文章體裁豐富多樣

廣納各類生活中**常見的體裁**，包含**短文、詩篇、對話、廣告、網站、新聞、短片、專欄**等，讓讀者學會閱讀多種體裁文章，將閱讀知識及能力應用於生活中。

## 4. 外師親錄課文朗讀 MP3

全書文章皆由專業外師錄製 MP3，示範正確發音，促進讀者聽力吸收，提升英文聽力與口說能力。

# Structure of the Book 本書架構

## Unit 1 閱讀技巧 Reading Skills

本單元訓練讀者**理解文意**的基本技巧，內容包含：

**❶ 歸納要旨／找出支持性細節 Main Ideas / Supporting Details**

**要旨**是文章傳達的關鍵訊息，也就是作者想要講述的重點。一般而言，只要看前幾句就能大略掌握文章的要旨。

**支持性細節**就像是築起房屋的磚塊，幫助讀者逐步了解整篇文章要旨，**事實**、**描述**、**比較**、**舉例**都能是支持性細節的一種。

**❷ 理解因果關係／釐清寫作技巧 Cause and Effect / Clarifying Devices**

一起事件通常都有發生的**原因**與造成的**結果**，讀者可以從文章內的 **because of**（由於）、**as a result of**（因而）等片語找出原因，並從 **as a result**（結果，不加 of）、**resulting in**（因此）和 **so**（所以）等片語得知結果。

作者會想讓自己的文章盡量引人入勝且文意明瞭。當你在閱讀時，需注意作者用哪些技巧達到此目的。看看作者是否提供事實及數據？是否向讀者提問？是否舉出例證？仔細閱讀每個句子及段落，試著分辨**寫作技巧**。

**❸ 作者的目的及語氣／做出推測**
**Author's Purpose and Tone / Making Inferences**

作者通常在寫作時有特定的**目的**，他可能是想博君一笑，或是引發你對某個主題深思。注意作者的**語氣**，他的語氣是詼諧、情感充沛亦或是有耐心的呢？作者的語氣可以幫助你找出作者的目的。

當你在進行**推測**時，需使用已知的資訊去推論出不熟悉的資訊。在篇章的上下文中，讀者藉由文中已提供的資訊去推測文意。

## Unit 2 字彙學習 Word Study

本單元訓練讀者**擴充字彙量**，並學會了解文章中的生字，內容包含：

**❶ 同義詞與反義詞 Synonyms / Antonyms**

在英文中有時兩字的意思相近，此時稱這兩字為**同義詞**；若兩字意思完全相反，則稱為**反義詞**。舉例來說，good（好）和 brilliant（很棒）的意思相近，為同義詞，但 good（好）和 bad（壞）的意思相反，故為反義詞。學習這些詞彙有助提升字彙量，並增進閱讀與寫作能力。

**❷ 從上下文推測字義 Words In Context**

遇到不會的英文字，就算是跟單字大眼瞪小眼，也無法了解其字義，但若好好觀察此字的**上下文**，或許就能推敲出大略的字義。這項技巧十分重要，尤其有助讀者在閱讀文章時，即使遇到不會的生字，也能選出正確答案。

## Unit 3 學習策略 Study Strategies

**影像圖表**與**參考資料**常會附在文章旁，幫助讀者獲得許多額外重點，本單元引導讀者善用文章中的不同素材來蒐集資訊，內容包含：

**❶ 影像圖表 Visual Material**

**影像圖表**可以將複雜資訊轉換成簡單的**表格、圖表、地圖**等，是閱讀時的最佳幫手。要讀懂圖表，首先要閱讀**圖表標題與單位**，接著觀察**數值**，只要理解圖表的架構，就能從中得到重要資訊。

**❷ 參考資料 Reference Sources**

**參考資料**像是**字典、書籍索引**等，一次呈現大量資訊，能訓練讀者自行追蹤所需重點的能力，並提升讀者對文章的整體理解。

## Unit 4 綜合練習 Final Review

本單元綜合前三單元內容，幫助讀者回顧全書所學，並藉由文後綜合習題，來檢視自身吸收程度。

# How to Use This Book

## 1 多樣主題增添閱讀樂趣與知識

旅遊

安全

職涯

---

### 24 ⊻ Wave Rock

https://www.seeaustralia.com.au/western-australia/perth/day-trips/wave-rock

# A Wave Made of Rock

Western Australia > Perth > Day Trips

## Wave Rock

**1** What is a wave doing more than 300 km away from the ocean, you might ask? This wave is not made of water but rather of rock! Wave Rock is one of Western Australia's most amazing natural sights. It looks as if an **enormous** wave has been frozen in time. The "wave" is 15 meters tall and over 100 meters long. It is a mix of yellow, brown, and grey. These many **shades** make it appear as if sunlight is shining on the wave as it rolls forwards. Of course, this wave is going nowhere—in fact, it has been around for more than 60 million years.

**2 Best Time to Visit:**
Spring—when the area's many beautiful flowers are starting to open.

**3 Getting There:**
Wave Rock is a four hour drive (340 km) from Perth, the nearest city. You can join one of the many buses that leave **there** daily, or drive yourself using your own car.

**4 Extend Your Stay:**
There are plenty of things to do around Wave Rock. Just one kilometer to the north is the beautiful Lake Magic, where you can watch an amazing sunrise. There is also the fun Wildlife Park, where you can see kangaroos, deer, exotic birds, and many other interesting animals. Those planning to stay the night can do so at The Wave Rock Hotel.

068

---

⊻ broken bottle

## 12 Summertime Swimming

**1 Swimming in Lakes and Rivers Can Be Dangerous!**

It's summer! Many people want to go swimming outside. But swimming in lakes and rivers can be very dangerous. Last year, 120 people in this area had accidents or health problems from swimming in lakes and rivers. Here are some of the dangers that you need to know about:

**2** ⚠ **Sharp Objects in the Water**
Sharp objects like broken bottles on the lake or river floor can be difficult to see. If you step on one, you can really hurt yourself.

⚠ **Cold Shock**
Cold water drains your body of energy quickly. Your arms and legs may stop working, and it will be difficult to swim back to land. If no one is around to help, you could drown.

**Q QUESTIONS**

___ 1. Why was this poster written?
(A) To make people laugh.　(B) To help keep people safe.
(C) To tell people about an event.　(D) To help sell some items.

___ 2. If people pay attention to the poster, what will likely happen to the number 120 from the first paragraph?
(A) It will go up a little this year.　(B) It will go down this year.
(C) It will stay the same this year.　(D) It will double this year.

___ 3. What is the writer's tone throughout most of the article?
(A) Sad.　(B) Excited.　(C) Scared.　(D) Serious.

___ 4. What is the writer's tone in the last paragraph?
(A) Helpful.　(B) Angry.　(C) Loving.　(D) Funny.

042

---

## 30 A Master of Smells

⊻ A nose should be able to identify different smells.

**1** In any perfume company, the most important person is most certainly the nose. Though it sounds more like a body part than a job title, the "nose" is the person who *creates* a company's famous scents. In the same way that an artist creates a painting by **combining** different colors, a nose creates perfumes by combining different smells.

**2** Noses need to have a lot of knowledge, as well as an excellent sense of smell. They must be able to **identify** thousands of different smells and understand how they work together. They must also know how smells change over time and how they make people feel. When

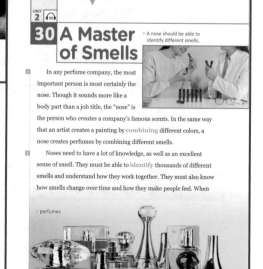

⊻ perfumes

080

---

014

## 2 多元體裁貼近日常閱讀體驗

詩篇

## 05 Father and Son

*"You don't understand me, Dad," I shout.*
*"You're old, and grumpy, and mean.*
*You've no idea what it's like to be me—*
*what it's like to be a teen!"*

*I stomp to my room, my face red with rage,*
*and I shut the door with a slam.*
*I hate him. I hate him. I hate him, I think.*
*He just doesn't get who I am.*

*We are two different species, from two different planets*
*Millions of light-years apart.*
*We're apples and oranges, cats and dogs.*
*He's science; I am art.*

*A knock at my door. My mother comes in,*
*and in her hands there's a book.*
*"Can I show you this?" she asks with a smile.*
*I shrug and agree to look.*

*I open it up—there are photos inside*
*of a young boy around my age.*
*He's laughing with friends and looking so cool*
*on page after page after page.*

*Here's one of him surfing at the beach.*
*Here's one of him playing guitar.*
*Here's one of him with his hair dyed green.*
*He looks like a young rock star!*

*"Who is this kid?" I ask my mother.*
*She says, "What? Don't you recognize the lad?"*
*I shake my head. I have no idea.*
*"That, my boy, is your dad!"*

≈ surfing

≈ green hair

028

海報

## 06 Calling All Students!

» science fair

### Pine View Junior High's
### 12th Annual Science Fair

Calling all students! Do you want to help save the planet? This year's Science Fair topic is "Taking Care of Our Planet." All students at Pine View may participate. Your project must present a change that our school can make to help the environment. Students can work alone, or in a group. Please note that students may only enter one project into the Science Fair. Students who enter more than one project will not be allowed to participate.

### How to Participate:

1. Complete the Science Fair Form.
2. Have the form signed by your science teacher.
3. Ask your parents to sign the form. For students working in groups, all parents must sign the form.
4. Give the form to your science teacher by April 18th.

This event will be on May 18th from 6 to 7 p.m. Students should come at 5:30 p.m. to set up in the library. Students must stay with their project during the fair. Students should also be ready to answer questions from the judges. Winners will be announced at 7 p.m.

030

網頁

» assembling a table

## 46 A New Table, Step by Step

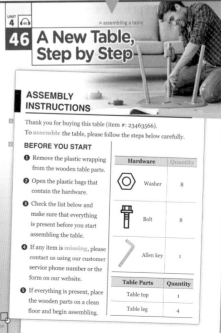

### ASSEMBLY INSTRUCTIONS

Thank you for buying this table (item #: 23463566).
To **assemble** the table, please follow the steps below carefully.

**BEFORE YOU START**

1. Remove the plastic wrapping from the wooden table parts.
2. Open the plastic bags that contain the hardware.
3. Check the list below and make sure that everything is present before you start assembling the table.
4. If any item is **missing**, please contact us using our customer service phone number or the form on our website.
5. If everything is present, place the wooden parts on a clean floor and begin assembling.

| Hardware | | Quantity |
|---|---|---|
| ⬡ | Washer | 8 |
| 🔩 | Bolt | 8 |
| ⌐ | Allen key | 1 |

| Table Parts | Quantity |
|---|---|
| Table top | 1 |
| Table leg | 4 |

136

015

# 3 每篇文章後附五道閱讀理解題，訓練培養九大閱讀技巧，包含：

_____ 1. What is the writer's main point in the passage?

(A) Sometimes, other people do not notice when you have been working hard.

(B) Studying hard is good, but it is also important to take care of yourself.

(C) Being a hard worker is a great way to reach your study goals.

(D) Some people study so hard they become afraid to take time off.

**❶ 歸納要旨**

_____ 2. According to the writer, what can focusing too much on your studies do to you?

(A) Make you sick.　　(B) Make you rich.

(C) Make you happy.　(D) Make you calm.

**❷ 找出支持性細節**

_____ 2. Why did Ella and Kei's friendship end?

(A) Ella was mean to Kei.

(B) Kei was mean to Ella.

(C) Ella found a new friend.

(D) Kei found a new friend.

**❸ 理解因果關係**

_____ 3. What does the writer try to do in the fourth paragraph?

(A) Give the answer to a question.　(B) Explain how to do something.

(C) Make the reader feel surprised.　(D) Give an example of something.

**❹ 釐清寫作技巧**

_____ 1. What is the writer's tone in the final paragraph?

(A) Angry.　(B) Afraid.　(C) Funny.　(D) Excited.

**❺ 作者的目的及語氣**

_____ 2. What can we guess about the writer from the third paragraph?

(A) The writer is confident.　(B) The writer is shy.

(C) The writer is not friendly.　(D) The writer is not very smart.

**❻ 做出推測**

_____ 2. Which of these words from the first paragraph has a similar meaning to "gesture"?

(A) Show.　(B) Person.　(C) Action.　(D) Tradition.

**❼ 了解同義字**

_____ 3. Which of these words has the opposite meaning to "ancient"?

(A) Modern.　(B) Difficult.　(C) Common.　(D) Important.

**❽ 了解反義字**

_____ 4. What does the writer mean by "this kind of person" in the second paragraph?

(A) Someone who grew up in India.

(B) Someone who is getting married.

(C) Someone who has better grades than you.

(D) Someone who is much older than you.

**❾ 從上下文推測字義**

# 4 各式圖表與全彩圖片促進閱讀理解

地圖

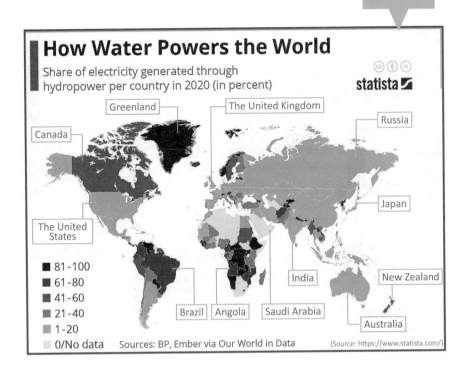

圖片

折線圖

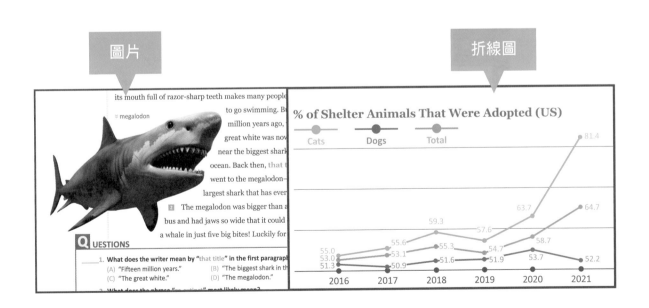

# UNIT
# 1

# Reading Skills

This unit covers six key elements you will need to focus on in order to properly understand an article: main idea(s), supporting details, cause and effect, clarifying devices, author's purpose and tone, and making inferences.

In this unit, you will learn how to understand what a text is mainly about, observe how details support main ideas, recognize connections between events, identify the way a writer makes their work interesting, pinpoint the reason behind an author's writing, and make assumptions based on information in the text.

>> vision board (cc by Debra Roby)

# 01 See it, Reach it!

**1** Do you have special goals you want to reach? Maybe you want to read a book a week. Maybe you want to be the top of your class or get on the school sports team. The thing is, reaching your goals can be hard. It is very easy to give up half way. One thing that can help is a vision board.

**2** A vision board is a collection of pictures that reflect your goals. Seeing the pictures every day keeps you focused. Here is how to make a vision board in four easy steps.

⌃ reaching a goal

**3** ## 1. Choose your goals

Choose a few goals that are important to you. They can be small goals, like drinking more water. Or they can be bigger goals, like learning a new language. For bigger goals, it helps to break them down into steps.

**4** ## 2. Find pictures

Look for pictures that reflect your goals. You can find these online and print them out. Or you can cut them out of old magazines and books.

**5** ## 3. Design your board

Stick your pictures to a board using tape or glue. You could also write some cheering words—like "Keep going!"—in the blank spaces.

**6** ## 4. Use it!

Put your board in a spot you look at every day, like your bedroom wall. Every morning, take a minute and focus on it. Think about your goals and what you are doing to reach them.

## UESTIONS

_____ 1. **Which of these does the writer think can be difficult?**

(A) Giving up on your goals.　　(B) Choosing your goals.

(C) Finding pictures online.　　(D) Reaching your goals.

_____ 2. **What is the writer's main point in the article?**

(A) People can have long-term goals and short-term goals.

(B) Making a vision board can help you reach your goals.

(C) You should look at your vision board every day.

(D) You can make a vision board in four easy steps.

_____ 3. **What is the main idea in step 1?**

(A) Drinking water is good for you, so you should do it more.

(B) For your vision board, choose goals that are important to you.

(C) Learning a new language takes lots of time and effort.

(D) You can reach big goals by taking small steps.

_____ 4. **Which of these places is a good place to put your vision board?**

(A)　　　　　　　(B)　　　　　　　(C)　　　　　　　(D)

_____ 5. **What does the writer suggest that you write in the blank spaces on your vision board?**

(A) Cheering words.　　　　(B) Your name and address.

(C) Things that make you sad.　　(D) Your favorite foods.

# 02 Strawberry Snack Bars for Sale

## MyTreat All Natural Snack Bars [Box]

☆☆☆☆☆　　　　　　　**Total reviews: 35**

**Total weight:** 228 grams

**Number of bars in each box:** 12

**Strawberry NT$900**　**Banana NT$900**

oat

dried fruit

**Order before March 31 and get free shipping!**

### About This Item

1　　MyTreat Snack Bars are healthy, delicious snack bars that you can enjoy for breakfast or for a snack during the day.

2　　We use all natural ingredients in our snack bars. We like to keep things simple, too. Our bars are made of three things only: dried fruit, honey, and oats. We never add any unnatural flavors. We believe that the best flavor always comes from using high-quality, natural ingredients. And we are 100% sure you will agree!

3　　We are also very careful about who we get our ingredients from. We only work with farmers who do not harm the environment. When you eat a MyTreat Snack Bar you can be sure that you are not supporting anyone who hurts our planet.

4　　Our snack bars give you a big boost whenever you are feeling low on energy. And they are just the right size to carry around with you in your bag. If you ever feel tired, just pull one out and take a bite! You'll have all the energy you'll need to make it through the rest of the day!

5　　Each box contains 12 snack bars. That works out at just NT$75 for each bar! So what are you waiting for? Give MyTreat a try!

# QUESTIONS

_____1. **How much does each box of MyTreat Snack Bars weigh?**

(A) Two hundred and eighteen grams.

(B) Two hundred and eight grams.

(C) Two hundred and eighty-two grams.

(D) Two hundred and twenty-eight grams.

_____2. **Which of these is NOT in a MyTreat Snack Bar?**

(A) Dried fruit.   (B) Honey.   (C) Oats.   (D) Milk.

_____3. **What do MyTreat Snack Bars say about the farmers they work with?**

(A) They don't harm the environment.

(B) They don't sell low-quality food.

(C) They are from all over the world.

(D) They only grow a small amount of food.

_____4. **What point is the writer trying to make in the fourth paragraph?**

(A) MyTreat Snack Bars fit easily into your bag.

(B) MyTreat Snack Bars give the people who eat them lots of energy.

(C) MyTreat Snack Bars are a convenient way to give yourself energy.

(D) MyTreat Snack Bars are good for people who get tired at work.

_____5. **Here is a review from someone who bought a box of MyTreat Snack Bars.**

> **GaryG**
>
> I bought a box of these snack bars last week. I have to say, they taste great and I enjoyed eating them. You can tell that the strawberries they use are of very high quality. But I think each bar was too small. One just wasn't enough, and each time I was hungry I had to eat two or three. I hoped that the box would last around two weeks, but after less than a week it is already empty. My advice to MyTreat: please make bigger bars!

**What is the writer's main point?**

(A) The writer bought a box of MyTreat Snack Bars last week.

(B) The strawberries used in MyTreat Snack Bars are of high quality.

(C) The snack bars are delicious but each one is too small.

(D) The writer wanted the box of snack bars to last for around two weeks.

# A Better Second Half?

« sports game broadcast

## SPORTS NEWS

**1** **Voice 1:** And here we are at the start of the second half. The score is currently East City two, South City zero. South City have a lot of work to do if they want to win this important game today.

**2** **Voice 2:** That's right. South City have been playing very poorly so far. Their defenders have been letting East City's forwards slip right past them, and their own forwards have not been very active at all. Hopefully, in this next half they can start to play more aggressively. I'm sure their coach, Mitch McDonald, had some harsh words for them during half time.

## QUESTIONS

_____1. **What is the main idea of the second paragraph?**
- (A) South City played poorly in the first half of the game.
- (B) South City need to play differently if they want to win the game.
- (C) South City are coached by Mitch McDonald.
- (D) South City's defenders need to work harder to stop East City scoring.

_____2. **What was the score at the end of the first half of the game?**
- (A) South City two, East City one.　　(B) East City two, South City one.
- (C) South City two, East City zero.　　(D) East City two, South City zero.

_____3. **What is the main idea of the final paragraph?**
- (A) South City just scored a fantastic goal.
- (B) South City need to score two more goals to win the game.
- (C) If South City keep playing this way, they could win the game.
- (D) Only a few minutes have gone by in the second half of the game.

_____4. **Who scored the goal for South City?**
- (A) Martins.　　(B) Smith.　　(C) Roberts.　　(D) Jones.

**3** **Voice 1:** Let's see if they paid attention to him. Here we go. South City kicks off. Brown has the ball. He passes it to Smith. Smith is now running up the field towards the East City goal, but here come the East City defenders! Roberts goes to tackle, but Smith dances around him.

**4** **Voice 2:** Wonderful play! Smith shows he has excellent skill with the ball. But can he get past Jones, the other defender, too? Smith and Jones, face to face now. Smith senses danger, so he passes the ball to Martins. Martins sees an opening. It's just him against the goalkeeper now. He shoots. He scores!

**5** **Voice 1:** A fantastic goal! In the opening minutes of the second half, South City have made it 2–1. What a change in performance! It's like they're a completely different team. If they keep playing like this, they might win the game after all!

» Skill of tackling in soccer games

⌃ goalkeeper

_____5. **Here is what Mitch McDonald, South City's coach, had to say at the end of the game.**

> In the second half, our forwards played very well and we scored two great goals. But East City's forwards were just too strong for our defenders in the end. Our defenders did their best, but by the end of the game they were too tired. And East City scored the winning goal in the last minute of the game. It was a sad end for us, but I'm proud of the way the team played.

**What is his main point?**
(A) South City's defenders were very tired by the end of the game.
(B) He is happy with how the team played even though they lost the game.
(C) East City scored the winning goal in the last minute of the game.
(D) He is sad his team did not win the game in the end.

» hardworking student

# Taking Care of You

**1**     Being a hardworking student is certainly a good thing. Sometimes, however, it is possible to get so focused on studying that you become afraid to take time off. Studying in this way can lead to ill health, so it is really important to include activities that help you relax as part of your routine. Here are three things you can do to keep your mind and mood healthy while working towards your study goals.

**2**     **1. Treat yourself** – People might not recognize your hard work, so they won't always reward you for it. However, it is important that *you* recognize your own efforts. When you know you have been studying hard, treat yourself to something nice, like enjoying a tasty dessert, spending time with friends, or playing a video game.

## Q UESTIONS

_____ 1. **What is the writer's main point in the passage?**
   (A) Sometimes, other people do not notice when you have been working hard.
   (B) Studying hard is good, but it is also important to take care of yourself.
   (C) Being a hard worker is a great way to reach your study goals.
   (D) Some people study so hard they become afraid to take time off.

_____ 2. **According to the writer, what can focusing too much on your studies do to you?**
   (A) Make you sick.      (B) Make you rich.
   (C) Make you happy.      (D) Make you calm.

_____ 3. **Which of these is a good way to "take some time out"?**
   (A) Start going to the gym.      (B) Eat out more often.
   (C) Read more books.      (D) Take a break from social media.

≪ rewarding yourself

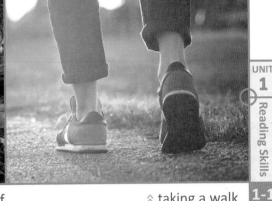
≪ taking a walk

**3** **2. Take some time out** – When you feel that the stress of studying is becoming too much, try to make time to switch off and relax. If you can't go on an actual vacation, try taking a break from social media. Cutting out all that "noise" will give you some much-needed space to breathe.

**4** **3. Take a walk** – Scientists have shown that walking lowers your stress levels, clears your head, and helps you sleep better. In short, walking just a little each day can have big benefits for your mental health.

**5** Hopefully, by doing these three simple things, you can reach your study goals while maintaining a healthy state of mind. Remember, while it is good to care about your studies, it is also important to care for yourself, too!

≫ a good night's sleep

_____4. **Which of these is NOT something the writer suggests you do after studying hard?**

(A)    (B)    (C)    (D)

_____5. **What is the main idea of point 3?**
(A) You will get a better night's sleep after taking a walk.
(B) Walking every day can help you feel calmer.
(C) Taking a walk can help you think more clearly.
(D) Taking a walk is a good way to keep your mind healthy.

# 05 Father and Son

⌃ surfing

⌃ green hair

"You don't understand me, Dad," I shout.
"You're old, and grumpy, and mean.
You've no idea what it's like to be me—
what it's like to be a teen!"

I stomp to my room, my face red with rage,
and I shut the door with a slam.
I hate him. I hate him. I hate him, I think.
He just doesn't get who I am.

We are two different species, from two different planets
Millions of light-years apart.
We're apples and oranges, cats and dogs.
He's science; I am art.

A knock at my door. My mother comes in,
and in her hands there's a book.
"Can I show you this?" she asks with a smile.
I shrug and agree to look.

I open it up—there are photos inside
of a young boy around my age.
He's laughing with friends and looking so cool
on page after page after page.

Here's one of him surfing at the beach.
Here's one of him playing guitar.
Here's one of him with his hair dyed green.
He looks like a young rock star!

"Who is this kid?" I ask my mother.
She says, "What? Don't you recognize the lad?"
I shake my head. I have no idea.
"That, my boy, is your dad!"

» father and son

# Q UESTIONS

_____1. **What is the writer's main point in the poem?**

(A) The speaker is not angry at his mother, but he is angry at his father.

(B) The speaker's mother has a book full of interesting photos.

(C) The speaker is wrong to think that his father doesn't understand him.

(D) The speaker thinks the kid in the photos looks like a rock star.

_____2. **What is the writer's main point in the first three verses?**

(A) The speaker thinks that science and art are opposites.

(B) The speaker thinks his father is mean.

(C) The speaker thinks he and his father are very different.

(D) The speaker wants to be alone in his room.

_____3. **What do we know about the boy in the photos?**

(A) He once changed his hair color.    (B) He was tall for his age.

(C) He liked to play video games.    (D) He did not have any friends.

_____4. **What is TRUE about the boy in the photos?**

(A) It is the speaker himself.    (B) The speaker has never met him.

(C) It is the speaker's father.    (D) The speaker's mother doesn't know him.

_____5. **Here are some notes from the writer's teacher about the poem.**

> A fun poem! I enjoyed this a lot. It made me laugh but also had something interesting to say about growing up. I think you could enter this for the school poetry prize next month. I think it would have a good chance of winning. I have one or two ideas about some small changes you could make, though. Stay for a few minutes after next class and we can talk about them. Great work!

**What is the teacher's main point in these notes?**

(A) The writer should come and see him after next class.

(B) He/She thinks the poem is good and could win a prize.

(C) He/She thinks the poem said interesting things about growing up.

(D) There are a few places where the writer could make some changes.

# 06 Calling All Students!

» science fair

## Pine View Junior High's
## 12th
## Annual Science Fair

**1**     Calling all students! Do you want to help save the planet? This year's Science Fair topic is "Taking Care of Our Planet." All students at Pine View may participate. Your project must present a change that our school can make to help the environment. Students can work alone, or in a group. Please note that students may only enter one project into the Science Fair. Students who enter more than one project will not be allowed to participate.

**2**
### How to Participate:

1. **Complete the Science Fair Form.**
2. **Have the form signed by your science teacher.**
3. **Ask your parents to sign the form. For students working in groups, all parents must sign the form.**
4. **Give the form to your science teacher by April 18th.**

**3**     This event will be on May 18th from 6 to 7 p.m. Students should come at 5:30 p.m. to set up in the library. Students must stay with their project during the fair. Students should also be ready to answer questions from the judges. Winners will be announced at 7 p.m.

« parents signing a form

↑ taking care of our planet

4 ## 1st Place

- Invitation to attend the City Science Fair in June
- $50 gift card to spend at our school cafeteria

5 ## 2nd Place

- Invitation to attend the City Science Fair in June
- $25 gift card to spend at our school cafeteria

6 ## 3rd Place

- Invitation to attend the City Science Fair in June

7     If you have any questions, please talk to your science teacher.

## Q UESTIONS

_____ 1. **Which of the following is the reading?**
   (A) A poster.    (B) A news article.
   (C) A report.    (D) A form.

_____ 2. **How does the writer create interest in the first paragraph?**
   (A) By stating the topic.
   (B) By asking a question.
   (C) By listing examples.
   (D) By making a funny joke.

_____ 3. **What does the phrase "Please note" do in the first paragraph?**
   (A) It emphasizes important information.
   (B) It introduces an example.
   (C) It expresses an agreement.
   (D) It introduces a next step.

_____ 4. **What will happen if students enter more than one form?**
   (A) They will need to get all forms signed by their parents.
   (B) They will not be allowed to participate.
   (C) They will need to arrive earlier to set up their projects.
   (D) They will be too busy to complete both projects.

_____ 5. **What will all students who win receive?**
   (A) A chance to set up their projects in the library.
   (B) Gift cards to spend at the school cafeteria.
   (C) A chance to answer questions from the judges.
   (D) Invitations to attend the City Science Fair.

UNIT
1
Reading Skills

1-2

Cause and Effect / Clarifying Devices

# 07 When Friendship Goes Bad

1. Not every friendship is for life.

2. Sometimes, friends just grow apart. This often happens as people get older and their interests change, or when one person moves away.

3. But other times, friendships end badly and mean things are said. This happened to Ella, 14, when she realized her "best friend" Kei wasn't such a nice person.

4. "We were at the park with some other girls," says Ella, "and Kei tried to cut me out of the group. Then she said something mean about my clothes, and everyone laughed. The next day, I told Kei she had upset me, but she didn't say sorry. In fact, she called me a loser."

5. The girls had been friends since second grade, so Ella found it painful to lose Kei. But she knew the friendship couldn't continue.

## Q UESTIONS

_____ 1. **According to the article, what is a reason friends grow apart?**
   (A) One person is smarter than the other.
   (B) They spend too much time together.
   (C) One person stops being honest.
   (D) They start to like different things.

_____ 2. **Why did Ella and Kei's friendship end?**
   (A) Ella was mean to Kei.
   (B) Kei was mean to Ella.
   (C) Ella found a new friend.
   (D) Kei found a new friend.

⌄ friendship gone bad

**6**     "Friends are meant to care for each other. I realized Kei wasn't a true friend anymore, but I missed her, and it took several months to make new friends. It was a lonely time."

**7**     If this happens to you, remember it is not the end of the world! When a friendship goes bad:

- Accept that not everything lasts forever.
- Understand your life is better without that mean person in it.
- Be thankful for the fun you had.

⌄ making new friends

- Think about the lessons you can learn from what happened.
- Keep telling yourself how great you are!
- Start spending time with other people as soon as you feel ready.

_____ 3. **What does the writer try to do in the fourth paragraph?**
     (A) Give the answer to a question.    (B) Explain how to do something.
     (C) Make the reader feel surprised.    (D) Give an example of something.

_____ 4. **What does the writer do at the last paragraph?**
     (A) Give some statistics.    (B) Give some pieces of advice.
     (C) Make a complaint.    (D) Raise a question.

_____ 5. **Why was Ella sad about losing Kei?**
     (A) Kei stopped answering her calls.
     (B) There wasn't a good reason for it.
     (C) They had been friends a long time.
     (D) Ella couldn't make any more friends.

# 08 A Very Hot Topic

**1** **Boy:** Gosh, I'm sweating like a pig today! The weather has been so hot recently.

**2** **Girl:** I think the temperature reached almost forty degrees earlier today. I'm very glad we have air conditioning at home.

**3** **Boy:** So am I. I really don't know how I would survive without air conditioning. Hey, did you know that in Europe hardly anyone has air conditioning in their homes?

**4** **Girl:** Don't they? But I saw in the news that the temperatures there are just as hot as they are here this summer.

**5** **Boy:** I actually asked my cousin who lives in the UK about this.

He said it's because until recently, they didn't really need it. Although the temperature did used to get hot in summer, it never got too hot to stand. The houses over there are usually designed to stay warm during the long, cold winters rather than be cool during the summer.

⌃ increasing temperatures

**6** **Girl:** That makes sense. But now with temperatures increasing each year I guess they are beginning to need air-conditioning.

**7** **Boy:** Yes, my cousin says more and more people are getting air conditioning now. His house just recently got it installed. He says he has it on twenty-four hours a day.

**8** **Girl:** You should tell him only use it if it gets dangerously hot. Otherwise, he will just get addicted to the cold air and end up using a lot of electricity. It's why my dad only lets us use it for a few hours every day when the temperature is at its hottest.

≋ air conditioning

≋ electricity

≋ hot summer

# **Q** UESTIONS

_____1. **Why is the boy sweating?**

(A) Because he has been exercising.

(B) Because he just ate some warm soup.

(C) Because the temperature is very high.

(D) Because he is sick.

_____2. **What does the boy do in the fifth paragraph?**

(A) Explain the reason for something.

(B) Give his opinion on something.

(C) Explain how to do something.

(D) Give an example of something.

_____3. **What is the effect of warmer weather in Europe?**

(A) More people are getting air conditioning for their homes.

(B) People are spending more time outside.

(C) Heat is killing more people than ever.

(D) People are spending less money on clothes.

_____4. **Why does the girl's family only use air conditioning for a few hours per day?**

(A) Because they like to use electric fans.

(B) Because they don't feel uncomfortable in warm weather.

(C) Because they don't want to waste electricity.

(D) Because not many people in Europe have air conditioning.

_____5. **How does the talk end?**

(A) With a funny joke.

(B) With a strange story.

(C) With a piece of advice.

(D) With an interesting question.

# 09 The Woman Behind Your Wi-Fi

HEDY LAMARR
ÖSTERREICH
ÖSTERREICHER IN HOLLYWOOD
55
TUMA 2011

⌃ Hedy Lamarr (1914–2000)

1 She was called "The Most Beautiful Woman in Film." However, Hedy Lamarr was so much more than a pretty face. Born in 1914, Lamarr was a famous American film actress. But she also loved inventing things. Even though she had no formal training in science, her ideas helped change the way we connect to the Internet. Without her, Wi-Fi might not exist!

2 Lamarr grew up as an only child, so she got a lot of attention from her father. He was very curious about technology. Together, they would talk for hours about how machines worked. As a result, Lamarr gained a strong interest in the subject. She even began taking apart her toys to see how they fit together.

3 Even though she later found fame as an actress, she still kept up her interest in inventing. During World War II, she and a friend developed a new method for hiding radio waves. The goal was to stop the enemy from interfering with radio-

↑ torpedo

» Wi-Fi

controlled torpedoes. However, **in the end**, the U.S. Navy did not use their ideas.

4    Sadly, many years went by before others began to see how important her work was. In time, however, her ideas would go on to inspire many modern technologies, including Wi-Fi. In 2014, 14 years after her death, Lamarr was finally entered into the National Inventors Hall of Fame for her great work.

# Q UESTIONS

_____ 1. **How does the writer create interest in the first paragraph?**
   (A) By making jokes.
   (B) By asking questions.
   (C) By giving several big numbers.
   (D) By saying surprising things.

_____ 2. **What does the writer mostly do in this passage?**
   (A) Explain how something works.
   (B) Give an answer to a problem.
   (C) Make the reader feel afraid.
   (D) Give facts about a person's life.

_____ 3. **Which of these was an effect of Lamarr's receiving a lot of attention from her father?**
   (A) She gained a strong interest in technology.
   (B) She became a famous film actress.
   (C) She had no formal training in science.
   (D) The U.S. Navy did not use her ideas.

_____ 4. **What was an effect of Lamarr's work on radio waves?**
   (A) It helped win World War II.
   (B) It made many scientists angry at her.
   (C) It changed the way we use the Internet.
   (D) It caused a lot of people to die.

_____ 5. **In the third paragraph, what do the words "in the end" show?**
   (A) An example will follow.
   (B) A result will follow.
   (C) A step will follow.
   (D) A question will follow.

## 10 Close Before Flushing!

» flushing the toilet

*Why you should always close the lid before you flush the toilet.*

By *Ryan Osman*

**1**      When you go to the bathroom, you probably follow a simple routine. First you do your business, then you flush the toilet, and finally, you wash and dry your hands. All done! Your hands are clean and your "business" is now far away in an underground pipe. Or is it? **Actually**, a thin layer of it is now covering *you* —all over your clothes, even your hair. It is also on your towels, your toothbrush, and on anything you took into the bathroom with you, like your phone.

**2**      But how on earth did it get there? Well, when you flush the toilet, the power of the flush sends tiny particles of whatever is in the bowl—for example, your poop—into the air. These particles have been shown to travel almost two meters away from the toilet! Disgusting, I know. And what if you share a bathroom with a sick person and then touch something that is covered in their poop? It turns out that flushing the toilet is an excellent way to spread diseases between people who live together.

**3**      So what can you do? **Luckily**, there is a solution. **Simply** close the toilet lid before you flush! Doing so keeps everything **safely** trapped in the toilet. It is still a good idea to disinfect your toilet lid once in a while. But the rest of your bathroom, as well as your clothes, hair, toothbrush, and phone, will **happily** stay poop-free!

« Closing the lid before flushing can prevent diseases spreading.

⌄ disinfecting the toilet

# Q UESTIONS

_____ 1. What does the word "actually" show in the first paragraph?

(A) A lie will follow.  (B) An example will follow.

(C) A similar thing will follow.  (D) A truth will follow.

_____ 2. Which of these is an effect of closing the lid when you flush the toilet, according to the article?

(A) You won't need to wash your hands.

(B) You won't have to clean the toilet so often

(C) Your bathroom won't be covered in poop.

(D) Your bathroom will smell better.

_____ 3. What is the second paragraph made up of?

(A) Questions and answers.  (B) Different ways to do something.

(C) A problem and solution.  (D) A list of important events.

_____ 4. What can happen if you don't shut the lid when you flush the toilet, according to the article?

(A) You can use the same towel for longer.

(B) You can save money on toothbrushes.

(C) People you live with can get sick.

(D) People you live with might start to waste water.

_____ 5. What word in the last paragraph shows that an easy rule will follow?

(A) Luckily.  (B) Simply.  (C) Happily.  (D) Safely.

# 11 A Whole New World of Books

» sharing opinions in class

Monday, March 14

**1**     Last month I wrote that I had joined a book club. Today was the first meeting. I read the book, which was called *The Long Road*. It is about a young boy's journey across America and set in the 1930s. It is totally unlike the books I usually read. Normally, I read scary stories about ghosts, vampires, and so on. But I actually enjoyed reading something so different. I love scary books. I have read a million of them! But I am excited now to read new kinds of stories.

**2**     I know, too, that by reading more widely I can discover things I never knew before. For example, by reading *The Long Road*, I learned a lot about American geography. And I got to see what life was like for people almost a hundred years ago.

**3**     I also loved how friendly everyone in the book club was. There were six others, and all of them were very welcoming and encouraged me to share my ideas. I think that by going to the meetings, I will grow a lot more confident about sharing my opinions and thoughts. And that will be great for when we have class discussions in school, because now I usually just let others talk.

**4**     Next month's book is one called *The Woman Who Stole the Moon*. I have already got a copy from the library. I can't wait to get started!

# Q UESTIONS

≫ book club

_____ 1. **What is the writer's tone in the final paragraph?**

(A) Angry.　　(B) Afraid.　　(C) Funny.　　(D) Excited.

_____ 2. **What can we guess about the writer from the third paragraph?**

(A) The writer is confident.　　(B) The writer is shy.

(C) The writer is not friendly.　　(D) The writer is not very smart.

_____ 3. **What is the main purpose of this piece?**

(A) To teach someone how to do something.

(B) To make someone change their mind.

(C) To record the writer's feelings about something.

(D) To make the writer feel better about something bad.

_____ 4. **What is probably TRUE about the writer?**

(A) The writer has never traveled across America.

(B) The writer prefers to buy books than borrow them from the library.

(C) The writer has read many books about American history.

(D) The writer won't be going to the book club meeting again.

_____ 5. **Here is the list of books for the book club's next five meetings.**

| Month | Book Title |
|---|---|
| April | *The Woman Who Stole the Moon* by Michael Tan |
| May | *The Thief of Paris* by Lily Hawkins |
| June | *My Family of Elephants* by Greg Green |
| July | *House of the Dead* by Stephanie Prince |
| August | *King of the Golden Castle* by Anne K. Jones |

**Which of these books has the writer most likely read already?**

(A) The book for May.　　(B) The book for June.

(C) The book for July.　　(D) The book for August.

UNIT 1 🎧 12

# 12 Summertime Swimming

» broken bottle

## 1 Swimming in Lakes and Rivers Can Be Dangerous!

It's summer! Many people want to go swimming outside. But swimming in lakes and rivers can be very dangerous. Last year, **120** people in this area had accidents or health problems from swimming in lakes and rivers. Here are some of the dangers that you need to know about:

### 2 ⚠ Sharp Objects in the Water

Sharp objects like broken bottles on the lake or river floor can be difficult to see. If you step on one, you can really hurt yourself.

### 3 ⚠ Cold Shock

Cold water drains your body of energy quickly. Your arms and legs may stop working, and it will be difficult to swim back to land. If no one is around to help, you could drown.

## Q UESTIONS

_____1. **Why was this poster written?**
(A) To make people laugh.
(B) To help keep people safe.
(C) To tell people about an event.
(D) To help sell some items.

_____2. **If people pay attention to the poster, what will likely happen to the number 120 from the first paragraph?**
(A) It will go up a little this year.
(B) It will go down this year.
(C) It will stay the same this year.
(D) It will double this year.

_____3. **What is the writer's tone throughout most of the article?**
(A) Sad.  (B) Excited.  (C) Scared.  (D) Serious.

_____4. **What is the writer's tone in the last paragraph?**
(A) Helpful.  (B) Angry.  (C) Loving.  (D) Funny.

≪ **blue-green algae**

**4**
**Blue-Green Algae**

These are bacteria that appear as large blue-green patches on top of the water. Swimming through these can hurt your skin and eyes.

**5**
**Poop in the Water**

Lakes and rivers contain lots of poop, from both humans and animals. If you swallow lake or river water, you may become very sick.

**6**
**Weil's Disease**

This is a disease spread by rats that pee in the water. It is a serious disease that can result in death.

**7** To avoid these dangers, please do not swim in any of our local lakes and rivers. Instead, why not visit one of our area's two swimming pools? There you can be sure of a safe, clean swimming experience!

_____5. **Jeff went swimming in a lake. Later he felt uncomfortable and went to see a doctor. Read the doctor's notes.**

| | |
|---|---|
| Patient's Name: | Jeff Jones |
| Date of Birth: | 12/12/1995 |
| Problem: | Went swimming this morning in a lake. Eyes are now red and sore. Skin feels like it's burning. |
| Medicine: | Eye drops, skin cream |

**What did Jeff most likely do?**
(A) Swallow some lake water.   (B) Get in the water when it was too cold.
(C) Step on something sharp.   (D) Swim through some blue-green algae.

# 13 A Gift for Mr. Huang

*Three students are chatting online.*

**Matt**

**Linda**

**Kiki**

Has everyone had a chance to think about what present we should get Mr. Huang before we graduate?

I thought we could get him a history book. We know he loves history.

Well, he teaches history. Don't you think getting him a history book is a little boring? I'm sure he has a million history books already.

Yes, I suppose you're right.

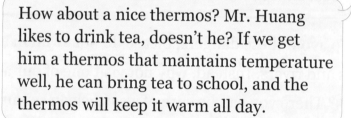
How about a nice thermos? Mr. Huang likes to drink tea, doesn't he? If we get him a thermos that maintains temperature well, he can bring tea to school, and the thermos will keep it warm all day.

## Q UESTIONS

_____1. **Who most likely is Mr. Huang?**
(A) He is one of the student's father.  (B) He is a worker at a bookstore.
(C) He is a local tea shop owner.  (D) He is a teacher at the students' school.

_____2. **What is Kiki's tone when she writes, "That's an excellent idea!"?**
(A) Positive.  (B) Nervous.  (C) Joking.  (D) Angry.

_____3. **Which of these is likely TRUE?**
(A) Two of the students do not want to talk about this topic today.
(B) Linda does not agree with the others' choice of gift.
(C) The three have talked about this topic before.
(D) Kiki wants to spend more than NT$1,500 on their gift.

**That's an excellent idea!**
He'll definitely love that. I'm looking online now. We can get a good thermos for around NT$1,000.

But the amount we agreed to spend previously was NT$1,500. Can we get him something else in addition to the thermos?

≫ thermos

Oh! I have an idea. There's a shop that sells tea near where I live. I could pick out a high-quality one for around NT$500. I think a thermos and a packet of good tea would make a nice gift set.

Excellent. So Kiki, you order the thermos; Linda, you buy the tea, and I'll write a card. Then we can all sign it and present everything to Mr. Huang on our final day.

_____ 4. **What is Matt's tone at the end of the chat?**

(A) Unhappy.　　(B) Decisive.　　(C) Excited.　　(D) Distant.

_____ 5. **After the chat, Linda visited the tea shop near her house. Which of the following items did she most likely buy?**

(A)　　　　　(B)　　　　　(C)　　　　　(D)

Price: NT$499　Price: NT$1,500　Price: NT$500　Price: NT$699

# 14 One Night at Oak Tree Hotel

— □ ✕

To: manager@oaktreehotel.com

From: dana.cook@fastmail.com

Subject: A terrible experience

Dear Sir/Madam,

**1**     I have recently returned home after staying at Oak Tree Hotel for one night. It was not a good experience. In fact, I have never had such a terrible experience at a hotel before.

**2**     The room was very dirty. There were dead flies on the floor, and after sleeping in the bed, my skin was very itchy the next day. I don't think the sheets had been cleaned in a long time. Also, there was loud music coming from the room next to mine. When I called the front desk to complain, I was told that there was nothing they could do about it. And when I ordered room service for dinner, the meal took over an hour to arrive, and it was ice cold!

**3**     I want to let you know that I will never be staying at this hotel again.

Dana Cook

## Q UESTIONS

_____1. **What is Dana Cook's tone in her email?**

(A) Joking.   (B) Gentle.   (C) Excited.   (D) Angry.

_____2. **What is the purpose of Dana Cook's email?**

(A) To give thanks for a great experience at Oak Tree Hotel.

(B) To book a room for one night at Oak Tree Hotel.

(C) To give others information about Oak Tree Hotel.

(D) To complain about a bad experience at Oak Tree Hotel.

_____3. **What is likely TRUE about the person who Dana spoke to on the phone during her stay?**

(A) The person had worked at the hotel for a long time.

(B) The person was not one of the hotel's regular workers.

(C) The person was in a great mood.

(D) The person couldn't hear what Dana was saying.

⌃ customer complaining　　　　⌃ room service　　⌃ dirty hotel room

_ □ ✕

To: dana.cook@fastmail.com

From: manager@oaktreehotel.com

Subject: Re: A terrible experience

Dear Ms. Cook,

**4**　　I am so sorry that you had a terrible experience at our hotel. Many of our staff have been sick recently, so we have a lot of temporary workers here at the moment. Unfortunately, they are not as well-trained as our regular staff.

**5**　　We will immediately refund you the cost of your room, and we hope you can forgive these mistakes.

**6**　　Also, for your information, most of our regular staff should be returning soon. We really hope you will stay with us again so that we can offer you a much better experience.

Yours sincerely,

Richard Jones, Manager

_____ **4. What is Richard Jones's tone in his email?**

(A) Sorry.　　(B) Happy.　　(C) Afraid.　　(D) Loving.

_____ **5. Shortly after receiving the reply from Richard Jones, Dana received a message on her phone. Which of these is likely that message?**

(A) From: **Oak Tree Hotel**
Thank you for booking two nights at Oak Tree Hotel. The total cost is $398.

(B) From: **City Bank**
This is to let you know that $199 has just been returned to you from Oak Tree Hotel.

(C) From: **Richard Jones**
Thank you for your email to Oak Tree Hotel. I am not at work right now, but I will reply as soon as possible.

(D) From: **Oak Tree Hotel**
Thank you for your dinner order. We will deliver it to your room when it is ready.

# 15 Changing Words, Changing Colors

**1**     Think of a rainbow. How many colors do you see? English speakers will see seven— red, orange, yellow, green, blue, indigo, and violet. However, speakers of the Dani language from Papua New Guinea would see only two colors—"mili" and "mola." The "warmer" part of the rainbow (red, orange, and yellow to English speakers) is "mili." The "colder" part (green, blue, etc.) is "mola." It is a strange and interesting fact: people can look at exactly the same colors, but *see* them differently depending on their language.

⌃ blueberries

**2**     Take another example. Picture the sky on a clear day and a blueberry. An English speaker would say, "They are both blue." One is light blue and the other dark blue, but still blue. A Greek speaker, on the other hand, would not agree. To the Greek, the sky is "ghalazio," while the blueberry is "ble." Two *totally different* colors! But there is a twist. Greeks who live in English-speaking countries start to see "ghalazio" and "ble" as being more and more similar over time. The "English" way of grouping these two colors as "blue" starts to *change the way they think*!

**3**     And this is not just true of color. Scientists have shown that language is related to the way we view space, numbers, and gender, to name but a few. This begs the question: do we or our words control how we think? At the end of the day, our thoughts may not be as free as we would like to imagine.

« rainbow    ⌃ the sky on a clear day

## **Q** UESTIONS

_____1. **What is the writer's purpose in this article?**
   (A) To show how Greeks are different from English people.
   (B) To make people want to spend more time outside.
   (C) To show how language affects the way people see colors.
   (D) To teach people about the science of rainbows.

_____2. **Why does the writer mention the Dani language in the first paragraph?**
   (A) To give an example.       (B) To give an opinion.
   (C) To make a joke.           (D) To make a guess.

_____3. **What might happen to an English speaker if they live for a long time in Greece?**
   (A) They will only see two colors when they look at a rainbow.
   (B) They will not be able to see the color red any more.
   (C) They will feel cold when they see the colors blue and green.
   (D) They will think of light blue and dark blue as separate colors.

_____4. **Which of these is likely the writer's opinion?**
   (A) The more languages you speak the smarter you become.
   (B) The language you speak has a big effect on your thoughts.
   (C) Speakers of the Dani language cannot create good art.
   (D) Words have no real effect on the way we think about the world.

_____5. **What is the writer's tone in the final paragraph?**
   (A) Bored.    (B) Excited.    (C) Kind.    (D) Serious.

# 16 Unlikely Partners

**1**  Mistletoe is a plant that lives by stealing food and water from large trees. Its seeds land on tree branches and then begin sucking out what they need to grow. But how do mistletoe seeds get up so high in the first place? They certainly can't fly! The answer: mistletoe uses a partner that *can* fly to place its seeds on high branches. This partner is known as the mistletoebird!

**2**  The mistletoebird, which can be found in Australia and parts of Indonesia, loves to eat mistletoe berries. These berries are protected by a thick skin. But, with its strong beak, the mistletoebird can easily tear a hole in the skin. It then pinches the fruit hard so that the delicious berry inside pops right out. For such a little bird, the large berry is a very satisfying meal.

**3**  The berry then passes through the bird's system. However, the seed at the center of the berry does not get broken down. After about thirty minutes, it pops out from the bird's other end whole and covered in a sticky goo.

≫ mistletoe berries
≫ mistletoe

« mistletoe seeds on a tree        ❯ mistletoebird

The bird then wipes its bottom on a branch to get rid of the sticky seed, which quickly puts down roots and starts to grow.

4      And then the cycle repeats. The mistletoe plant provides food for the mistletoebird, and the mistletoebird makes sure mistletoe seeds find a good place to grow. What a convenient partnership!

# **Q**UESTIONS

_____1. **How does mistletoe get food and water?**
   (A) It gets them from the mistletoebird.
   (B) It sucks them up from the earth.
   (C) It takes them from the air around it.
   (D) It steals them from large trees.

_____2. **What is the writer's purpose in the third paragraph?**
   (A) To explain how something happens.
   (B) To show how serious a problem is.
   (C) To make the reader feel excited.
   (D) To make the reader feel afraid.

_____3. **What is the first paragraph made up of?**
   (A) A funny story.          (B) Two different opinions.
   (C) A problem and answer    (D) A famous saying.

_____4. **What is the main point of the second paragraph?**
   (A) The mistletoebird gets a good, easy meal from the mistletoe plant.
   (B) The mistletoebird is a small bird, but it has a strong beak.
   (C) The mistletoebird is found in Australia and parts of Indonesia.
   (D) Mistletoe berries are protected by a thick skin.

_____5. **Which of these is an effect of mistletoe and the mistletoebird being partners?**
   (A) Neither is eaten by other animals.
   (B) Both get something they need to live.
   (C) Neither dies because of cold weather.
   (D) Both stay free of illnesses.

# 17 Dear Dad

Dear Dad,

**1**     Happy Father's Day! I wanted to write a note to tell you how grateful I am for all you do for me. Because of you I have a nice place to live and I never go hungry. I can focus on my school work without having to worry about anything else.

**2**     I know it's hard for you to take care of me by yourself and work a full-time job. I see how tired you are sometimes when you get home from work, but you never complain about having to help me with my homework. You always try hard to make time for me even though your job is very busy. I know this is very difficult, but I want you to understand how much I love spending time with you.

**3**     But from now on I want you to take better care of yourself, too. I will do my best to help with the housework and maybe cook dinner sometimes for us. That way you can relax a little more when you get home from work. I can also go and stay with grandma and grandpa some weekends so you can have a good rest and do things that you enjoy. You are very important to me, and I want you to be happy and healthy.

Lots of love,
Your son, Kyle

≈ Father's Day

≈ Dad helping his son
with homework

≈ doing the housework

# Q UESTIONS

_____ 1. **What is the writer's purpose in writing this card?**
   (A) To complain about something.
   (B) To show someone how to do something.
   (C) To thank someone for something.
   (D) To stop someone from getting hurt.

_____ 2. **What is likely TRUE about Kyle?**
   (A) His father works in a school.
   (B) He has a younger brother.
   (C) His grandparents live far away.
   (D) His mother is not around.

_____ 3. **Which of these is TRUE about Kyle's father?**
   (A) He only works on weekends.
   (B) He works until late at night.
   (C) His job is not very busy.
   (D) He works full time.

_____ 4. **How does the writer start the third paragraph?**
   (A) With a joke.
   (B) With a wish.
   (C) With an example.
   (D) With a question.

_____ 5. **What is the main idea in the third paragraph?**
   (A) Kyle wants to do things to help keep his father happy and healthy.
   (B) Kyle will help with the housework from now on.
   (C) Kyle's father is a very important person in Kyle's life.
   (D) Kyle's father should not forget to take care of himself.

# 18 Powerful Colors

**1**     Can our moods and behavior be affected by the colors around us? Many people think so. Some people like to paint their bedrooms blue because they believe the color is calming. Fast-food restaurants are often painted red and yellow. This is because red is thought to make you feel hungry and yellow to make you feel happy and friendly. Prison cells in some countries are painted pink because pink is thought to make people less likely to want to fight.

**2**     It is easy to think of reasons why these colors might make people act in certain ways. Blue, for example, likely makes people think of a clear sky on a beautiful summer's day or the peaceful ocean. Red is the color of many ripe fruits, such as apples, strawberries, and tomatoes. When you think about it like this, it certainly makes a lot of sense.

**3**     Scientists have tried to prove these ideas many times in tests. However, the results are never very reliable. Whenever a test "proves" that a color affects people in a certain way, a similar test, done later, disproves it. What, then, is the real truth of the situation?

**4**     It could simply be that the way colors affect each of us is highly individual, and there is no general rule. Better tests are now being designed to get to the bottom of this. But it may still be a while before we know the truth about why and how colors affect us, or even if they do at all.

› Fast-food restaurants are often painted red and yellow.

› In some countries, prisons are painted pink to make prisoners less likely want to fight.

# Q UESTIONS

_____1. **What is the first paragraph mostly made up of?**

(A) Numbers.　　(B) Questions.　　(C) Problems.　　(D) Examples.

_____2. **What is the writer's main point in the third and fourth paragraphs?**

(A) Many tests have been done to see how colors affect us.

(B) The way colors affect us might be highly individual.

(C) New tests are being designed to help us find out how different colors affect us.

(D) Even after many tests, we still don't know why, how, or if colors affect us.

_____3. **According to the second paragraph, what does the color blue likely make people think of?**

(A) A fast sports car.　　　　　　(B) A clear sky.

(C) Social media.　　　　　　　　(D) A person's eyes.

_____4. **What is the writer's attitude at the end of the second paragraph?**

(A) Agreeing.　　(B) Bitter.　　(C) Worried.　　(D) Comic.

_____5. **Jack split his class in half to do a test. To one half he offered 30 cookies from a blue plate, and to the other, 30 cookies from a red plate. After 10 minutes, he counted how many cookies had been eaten from each plate. Here are the results:**

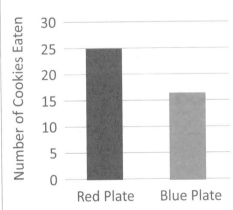

**Red/Blue Plate Test**

Number of Cookies Eaten

**Which idea from the article does the result of Jack's test seem to support?**

(A) Fast-food restaurants are often painted in red and yellow.

(B) Red is the color of many ripe fruits.

(C) The color red makes you feel hungry.

(D) The results of color tests are almost never reliable.

# 19 With This, Almost Anything Is Possible

**1**     Self-discipline is one of the greatest skills a person can have. What does self-discipline mean? It means being able to control yourself and your behavior. It means being able to do the right thing and avoid bad habits, such as wasting time. For students, this means finishing your homework before you play video games. It means paying attention in class when it might be more fun to talk secretly with your friends. It means putting away your phone and reading that important book.

⌃ self-discipline

**2**     But let's be honest, self-discipline is not easy. Bad habits can often be very difficult to resist. Indeed, to be self-disciplined you need a strong mind.

## Q UESTIONS

_____ 1. **What is the main idea of the passage?**
(A) Self-discipline is a great skill that can change your life for the better.
(B) Theodore Roosevelt thought self-discipline was very important.
(C) Bad habits can often be very difficult to resist.
(D) Self-discipline means being able to do the right thing and avoid bad habits.

_____ 2. **Which of these is TRUE about self-discipline?**
(A) Most people are born with it.
(B) It can be developed with practice.
(C) It is taught in schools in the United States.
(D) Students don't usually find it very helpful.

⌃ finishing your homework
before playing video games

⌃ Smartphones can be a distraction
when you're trying to focus.

No one is born with strong self-discipline, but it is something that you can develop. You do this the same way you get good at a sport or playing an instrument—with practice.

**3**   A good way to begin is to focus on something small, like getting up at the same time every day. Then, bit by bit, set yourself more difficult challenges. Take note, too, of your strengths and weaknesses. Figure out what makes you distracted (maybe it's having your phone by your side) and what makes you feel motivated (perhaps it's listening to music). Use this knowledge to help you build your self-discipline.

**4**   As your self-discipline grows, you should begin to feel more in control of yourself. You will begin to succeed more and goals that seemed impossible will suddenly seem within reach. As the great President of the United States Theodore Roosevelt once said, "With self-discipline, almost anything is possible!"

_____3. **How does the writer end the first paragraph?**
   (A) With numbers.       (B) With advice.
   (C) With examples.       (D) With a problem.

_____4. **According to the writer, having good self-discipline will help you do which of the following?**
   (A) Play more video games.        (B) Listen to more music.
   (C) Spend more time on your phone.   (D) Reach more goals.

_____5. **What is the writer's tone at the end of the passage?**
   (A) Comic.   (B) Cheering.   (C) Tired.   (D) Worried.

# 20 Bring a Cup, Save the Planet

**1** Our next story this evening is about the environment, and the positive steps many beverage stores are taking to reduce waste. **2** We all know how much garbage is created by buying drinks that come in plastic or paper cups. Therefore, in order to get to zero waste, many coffee shops and drinks vendors around the country are offering discounts to customers who bring their own cup.

**Charles Smith**
**Owner, King Coffee**

**3** We don't want to contribute to polluting our planet. So at the start of the year, we started offering drinks at 10% off to customers who bring their own cup. Since then, the number of cups we give out has dropped by 25%, which is a great result. Of course, we are hoping that it will drop even further.

**Olivia Ali**
**Regular Buyer**

4     I buy coffee in the morning on the way to work, and then I'll buy some milk tea on my way home. I never used to bring my own cup. But after lots of places started offering discounts for bringing your own cup, I went out and bought a reusable one. Now I take it with me when I go to buy a drink. Every day, I save money, and I'm doing my bit to save the planet. It feels great!

5     After learning about these actions, the government is now working to get more stores to do the same. We will keep following this story over the coming months.

_____ 1. **Which of these best describes the article?**
(A) Instructions.    (B) Life story.
(C) News.           (D) Advice.

_____ 2. **What is Charles Smith doing to try to cut waste?**
(A) Giving a free gift to people who bring their own cup.
(B) Selling drinks cheaper to those who bring their own cup.
(C) Only selling drinks in cups that can be recycled.
(D) Making people buy coffee on their way to work.

_____ 3. **What is Olivia Ali's tone at the end of her speech?**
(A) Comic.       (B) Pleased.
(C) Worried.    (D) Formal.

_____ 4. **According to Olivia Ali, which of these is an effect of her bringing her own cup when she buys a drink?**
(A) She is spending less money.
(B) She has to get up earlier in the morning.
(C) She feels bad for the planet.
(D) She buys milk tea every day.

_____ 5. **What does the government most likely think about the actions of Charles Smith and others like him?**
(A) They are bad for the planet.
(B) They won't have any effect.
(C) They are a great idea.
(D) They are harmful for people.

# UNIT
# 2

# Word Study

In this unit, you will practice identifying words with the same or opposite meanings, and guessing the meanings of words from their context. These skills will help you understand new vocabulary and build vocabulary on your own in the future.

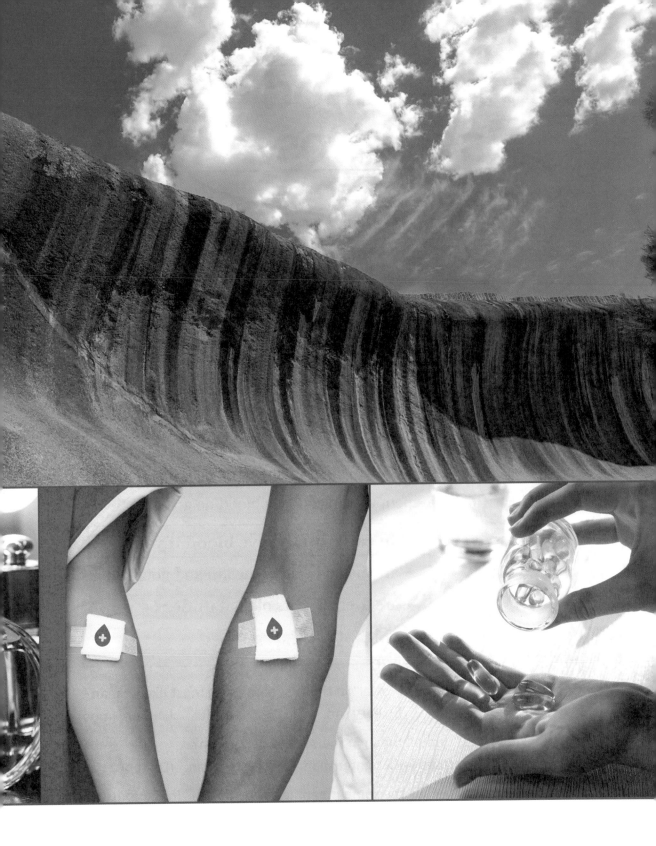

# 21 Give Blood, Save Lives

# GIVE BLOOD, SAVE LIVES

**1** | **Why should you give blood?**

Blood is **vital** for saving people's lives. It helps people survive serious accidents, surgeries, and even cancer. Hospitals need a lot of it. They also need all blood types. But right now, only 3% of people who can give blood do give blood.

**2** | **You can usually give blood if you . . .**

- are in good general health and not feeling sick
- are over 16 years old but **under** 65
- weigh at least 50 kg

⌃ blood donation

# Q UESTIONS

_____ **1.** What does the word "vital" in the first paragraph most likely mean?

(A) Not healthy.    (B) Very sad.    (C) Not useful.    (D) Very important.

_____ **2.** What does "under" mean in the second paragraph?

(A) Younger than.    (B) Lighter than.    (C) Faster than.    (D) Shorter than.

_____ **3.** Which of these has the same meaning as "complete" in the fourth paragraph?

(A) Take out    (B) Give up.    (C) Fill in.    (D) Hand over.

_____ **4.** Which of these is the opposite of "take it easy" in the final paragraph?

(A) Exercise.    (B) Sit.    (C) Drink.    (D) Rest.

## 3 Preparing to give blood

- Get a full night's sleep.
- Do not take any medicine for at least 24 hours before.
- Have a good meal, but avoid fatty foods.
- Drink lots of water.

## 4 The process of giving blood

1. Show your ID and **complete** your blood donor form.
2. Have your blood type checked.
3. Get weighed.
4. Answer some questions from a doctor.
5. Give blood (this takes around 10 minutes).

Go online to find the nearest place where you can give blood:

www.giveblood.com

## 5 What to do after you give blood

- **Take it easy** for 5-10 minutes.
- Right away, drink some water and eat a snack.
- Do not do any difficult exercises for the rest of the day.
- Do not take a hot bath or shower.
- Lie down immediately if you feel dizzy.
- Eat some iron-rich food for your next meal.

_____5. **Kevin wants to give blood, so he visited the website mentioned on the poster. What is another word for "selected"?**

(A) Ignored.
(B) Chosen.
(C) Visited.
(D) Sold.

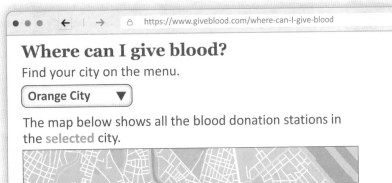

https://www.giveblood.com/where-can-I-give-blood

### Where can I give blood?

Find your city on the menu.

Orange City ▼

The map below shows all the blood donation stations in the **selected** city.

# 22 A Simple but Important Touch

**1**     Perhaps you've seen the action in a Bollywood movie or TV show set in India—a young person bends down and touches an elder's feet. For people not familiar with Indian traditions, this might seem like a weird thing to do. What does this gesture mean? Why touch the feet and not, say, the hands?

**2**     The tradition of touching an elder's feet is an ancient one. In fact, it started around 3,000 years ago! For Hindus, of which there are over a billion in India, it is a sign of deep respect. The action of bending down, sometimes kneeling or even lying, puts you in a lower position than the elder. Being in this position shows you recognize that this kind of person has more experience and wisdom than you do.

**3**     In return for the gesture, you receive a blessing from the elder. Touching an elder's feet is an important act for those who are seeking

» Touching the feet of one's parents is a tradition in Hindu wedding ceremonies.

>> A child touches an elder's feet to show respect.

wisdom, good health, or good luck. As a result, Hindus will often touch an elder's feet during important occasions, such as birthdays and weddings. They may also seek blessings in this way before difficult tasks, such as going on a long journey or taking an exam.

4     The tradition is taught to children from an early age. As a result, most Indians grow up with lots of respect for their elders. It may just be a simple action, but it certainly teaches a very important lesson to India's **youth**.

## Q UESTIONS

_____ 1. **What is another word for "weird" in the first paragraph?**
   (A) Fast.     (B) Strange.    (C) Loving.     (D) Calm.

_____ 2. **Which of these words from the first paragraph has a similar meaning to "gesture"?**
   (A) Show.     (B) Person.    (C) Action.     (D) Tradition.

_____ 3. **Which of these words has the opposite meaning to "ancient"?**
   (A) Modern.   (B) Difficult.   (C) Common.   (D) Important.

_____ 4. **What does the writer mean by "this kind of person" in the second paragraph?**
   (A) Someone who grew up in India.
   (B) Someone who is getting married.
   (C) Someone who has better grades than you.
   (D) Someone who is much older than you.

_____ 5. **Which of these words from the final paragraph has a similar meaning to "youth"?**
   (A) Elders.     (B) Children.   (C) Lessons.    (D) Respect.

# 23 Counting the Roman Way

⌃ Some clocks use Roman numerals.

**1**     Look at the faces of some clocks and you'll notice that the hours are not represented by 1, 2, 3, 4, and so on. Rather, they are shown by the symbols I, II, III, IV . . . . "Why are they written in this strange way?" you might **wonder**. It is because the numbers on clocks are often written using *Roman* numerals.

**2**     Roman numerals are how numbers were written in ancient Rome, around two thousand years ago. For modern people, the system can be a little **tricky** to understand, but with practice it gets easier. First, just remember that a value of one is shown by the letter I, five by the letter V, and 10 by the letter X. Next, it follows that two is written as "one plus one," or II, four as "one less than five," or IV. Similarly, six is "five plus one," or VI, and nine is "one less than ten," or IX. Finally, 11 is "10 plus 1," or XI, and so on. It is thought that these numerals were invented by **shepherds** as a way to count their sheep. For each sheep, they made a cut into a piece of wood (I). Every fifth sheep got two cuts (V), and every tenth a cross (X).

**3**     Today we seldom use Roman numerals to count. Indeed, there are some **flaws** in the system, one being there is no symbol for zero. However, **they** are still used occasionally. For example, you might see them marking chapter numbers in books or dates on old buildings and statues. Now, when you see these strange symbols, they'll no longer be a mystery.

# Roman Numerals

| | | | |
|---|---|---|---|
| 1 = I | 10 = X | 100 = C | 1000 = M |
| 2 = II | 20 = XX | 200 = CC | 2000 = MM |
| 3 = III | 30 = XXX | 300 = CCC | 3000 = MMM |
| 4 = IV | 40 = XL | 400 = CD | |
| 5 = V | 50 = L | 500 = D | |
| 6 = VI | 60 = LX | 600 = DC | |
| 7 = VII | 70 = LXX | 700 = DCC | |
| 8 = VIII | 80 = LXXX | 800 = DCCC | |
| 9 = IX | 90 = XC | 900 = CM | |

⌃ old building with Roman numerals

# **Q**UESTIONS

_____1. **What is another word for "wonder" in the first paragraph?**

  (A) See.      (B) Think.      (C) Write.      (D) Count.

_____2. **What is the opposite of "tricky" in the second paragraph?**

  (A) Simple.   (B) Difficult.   (C) Old.      (D) New.

_____3. **Which of these pictures shows a "shepherd"?**

(A)      (B)

(C)      (D)

_____4. **What is another way to say "flaw" in the final paragraph?**

  (A) Weak point.              (B) Far-away place.

  (C) Long time.               (D) Good way.

_____5. **What does "they" refer to in the final paragraph?**

  (A) Modern people.           (B) Ancient Romans.

  (C) Roman numerals.          (D) Old buildings.

# A Wave Made of Rock

Western Australia > Perth > Day Trips

## Wave Rock

**1**    What is a wave doing more than 300 km away from the ocean, you might ask? This wave is not made of water but rather of rock! Wave Rock is one of Western Australia's most amazing natural sights. It looks as if an **enormous** wave has been frozen in time. The "wave" is 15 meters tall and over 100 meters long. It is a mix of yellow, brown, and grey. These many **shades** make it appear as if sunlight is shining on the wave as it rolls forwards. Of course, this wave is going nowhere—in fact, it has been around for more than 60 million years.

**2** **Best Time to Visit:**
Spring—when the area's many beautiful flowers are starting to open.

**3** **Getting There:**
Wave Rock is a four hour drive (340 km) from Perth, the nearest city. You can join one of the many buses that leave **there** daily, or drive yourself using your own car.

**4** **Extend Your Stay:**
There are plenty of things to do around Wave Rock. Just one kilometer to the north is the beautiful Lake Magic, where you can watch an amazing sunrise. There is also the fun Wildlife Park, where you can see kangaroos, deer, exotic birds, and many other interesting animals. Those planning to stay the night can do so at The Wave Rock Hotel.

☆ Lake Magic, near Hyden, Western Australia (cc by Lawrence Murray)

☆ exotic bird

_____1. **What is the opposite of "enormous" in the first paragraph?**
(A) Large.    (B) Small.
(C) Great.    (D) Weak.

_____2. **What is another word for "shades" in the first paragraph?**
(A) Colors.    (B) Times.
(C) Roads.    (D) Stones.

_____3. **What does the writer mean by "there" in the third paragraph?**
(A) Western Australia.
(B) Wave Rock.
(C) Perth.
(D) Lake Magic.

_____4. **What does the word "extend" in the final paragraph most likely mean?**
(A) Make something shorter.
(B) Make something more difficult.
(C) Make something longer.
(D) Make something easier.

_____5. **If you click on the link for "The Wave Rock Hotel," you are shown this information. What is another way to say "make a reservation"?**

---

● ● ●

**Wave Rock Hotel**

*3-star hotel. Simple rooms, two restaurants, and a swimming pool.*
Address: 2 Lynch St, Hyden WA 6359
To **make a reservation**,
call: +61 8 9780 5048

---

(A) Book a room.    (B) Take a photo.
(C) Cook a meal.    (D) Drive a car.

# 25 King of the Sharks

**1**     Today, the great white is the world's largest shark. It can grow to be over six meters in length. And just the thought of its mouth full of razor-sharp teeth makes many people scared to go swimming. But 15 million years ago, the great white was nowhere near the biggest shark in the ocean. Back then, **that title** went to the megalodon—the largest shark that has ever lived!

❯ megalodon

**2**     The megalodon was bigger than a bus and had jaws so wide that it could eat a whale in just five big bites! Luckily for us,

## Q UESTIONS

_____1. **What does the writer mean by "that title" in the first paragraph?**
(A) "Fifteen million years."      (B) "The biggest shark in the ocean."
(C) "The great white."      (D) "The megalodon."

_____2. **What does the phrase "go extinct" most likely mean?**
(A) Totally disappear.      (B) Grow in number.
(C) Get eaten by another animal.      (D) Move to a different area.

_____3. **What does the phrase "play a major role" most likely mean?**
(A) Have only a small effect on something.
(B) Make something more difficult.
(C) Have an important part in something.
(D) Make something happen more slowly.

_____4. **Which of these is the opposite of "shrank" in the third paragraph?**
(A) Died.      (B) Rose.      (C) Slimmed.      (D) Grew.

« megalodon tooth *(left)* vs. great white shark tooth *(right)*

the megalodon **went extinct** about 3.5 million years ago. Can you imagine how dangerous it would be to swim, surf, or operate a boat with that kind of monster swimming around?

**3** So why did this king of the sharks disappear from the oceans? It was likely due to several reasons, but climate change **played a major role**. The megalodon lived and hunted in warm waters. Around five million years ago, however, the earth's temperatures began to drop. The oceans became colder, and the areas in which the megalodon could live **shrank**. What's more, this cooling caused many other animals to die out, too—animals that the megalodon relied on for food. In such conditions, the megalodon just could not survive.

**4** Now, all that is left of these ocean giants are fossils of their 18-centimeter-long teeth, which sometimes wash up on the shore.

_____ 5. **What is another word for "massive" in the chart below?**

**How massive was the megalodon?**

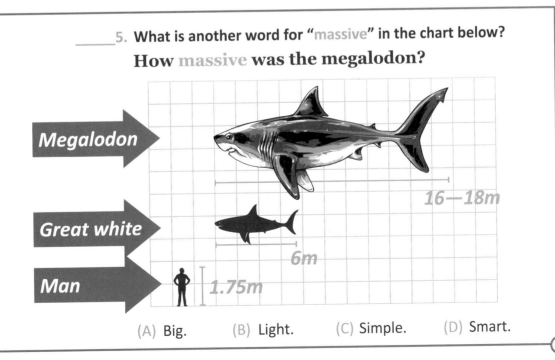

Megalodon

16—18m

Great white

6m

Man

1.75m

(A) Big.　　(B) Light.　　(C) Simple.　　(D) Smart.

# 26 Putting Feelings Into Words

» Not allowing boys to cry could cause them to act more violently.

**1**    "Boys don't cry!" is something young boys are often told when they get upset. While girls are **permitted** to express their emotions freely, boys are often taught from a young age to shut their feelings up inside.

⌃ Boys are taught from a young age that they should not cry.

**2**    However, holding in your feelings can cause problems with mental health later in life. It can also cause young men to act more violently as they have no other way to express themselves. Boys are sometimes told they are weak if they try to express their emotions, but this isn't true. It takes a lot of courage to express how you truly feel. Furthermore, **doing so** can make you feel more understood and in control of yourself. In short, it is a *very* positive thing.

**3**    So how do you do it? The first step is to take some time to think about exactly what emotion you are feeling. Try to be as **specific** as possible. Then try to think about *why* you are feeling that way. When you have the complete thought in your head, say it **aloud**. If you are not used to expressing your feelings, this can be difficult, but it will come with practice. Also, be sure to express your positive feelings as

« Expressing feelings is a positive thing.

well as your negative ones. Expressing positive feelings can help you build stronger connections with those you love and make you feel better about yourself.

4 When you think about it, it seems silly to miss out on these excellent benefits just because you are a boy. So express yourself, no matter your gender! You certainly won't regret it!

# QUESTIONS

_____ 1. **What is another word for "permitted" in the first paragraph?**
(A) Prevented. (B) Regretted. (C) Believed. (D) Allowed.

_____ 2. **What does the writer mean by "doing so" in the second paragraph?**
(A) Acting violently to people. (B) Making yourself understood.
(C) Expressing your emotions. (D) Holding in your feelings.

_____ 3. **What is the opposite of "specific" in the third paragraph?**
(A) General. (B) Lazy. (C) Lonely. (D) Personal.

_____ 4. **What is the opposite of "aloud" in the third paragraph?**
(A) Beautifully. (B) Bravely. (C) Silently. (D) Carefully.

_____ 5. **What is another word for "silly" in the final paragraph?**
(A) Foolish. (B) Cruel. (C) Kind. (D) Wise.

# 27 Get Ready for the Three Trees Book Fair

**March 2–4, 2023**
10 a.m.–4 p.m.

## Three Trees Books Is Coming to Hilltown School

**1**     We are very excited to announce the 2023 Three Trees Book Fair! We invite students of Hilltown School to visit our book tent, which will be set up on the school soccer field. Choose from hundreds of amazing books by some of the world's best **authors**.

**2**     What do you like to read? Exciting space adventures with aliens on far-away planets? Ghost stories set in spooky houses? **Tales** of two people falling in love? Travel diaries from interesting **foreign** places? We have all these and much more!

## QUESTIONS

_____ 1. **What is another word for "authors" in the first paragraph?**
(A) Readers.    (B) Sellers.    (C) Buyers.    (D) Writers.

_____ 2. **What is another word for "Tales" in the second paragraph?**
(A) Students.    (B) Coins.    (C) Stories.    (D) Events.

_____ 3. **Which of these is the opposite of "foreign" in the second paragraph?**
(A) Frightening.    (B) Boring.    (C) Local.    (D) Expensive.

_____ 4. **What does "everything" in the final paragraph most likely mean?**
(A) All books.    (B) All forms.    (C) All subjects.    (D) All news.

⌃ **book fair**

3    To see a list of all our books before you visit the fair, go to our website www.threetreespublishing.com/book-list. There, you can find information about all our titles.

4    If you would like to reserve a book, ask your teacher for a "Book Request Form." Fill it in with the book's information, and return it to your teacher. This way, you can be sure that the books you really want to buy will be at the fair.

5  **Some more good news!**

Because we love encouraging young people to read, we will be selling **everything** at 20% off! So come along and check out our books. You might just discover a new favorite!

_____5. **Jenna wants to buy a book at the book fair, so she asked her teacher for a Book Request Form. Which of these is another word for "details"?**
(A) Date.
(B) Cost.
(C) Information.
(D) Number

**BOOK REQUEST FORM**

**Student** Details
Name: Jenna Boyd
Class: 9A

**Book Details**
Title: The Lost World
By: Anna Keys
Code: AC9283SSF

# 28 Sleeping Well to Stay Alert

**1**   It is a fact—getting too little sleep is one of the worst things you can do for your health. Studies have shown that **it** can lead to all kinds of serious health problems, such as heart attacks and cancer. However, few people realize just how seriously lack of sleep can affect your brain on a daily basis.

**2**   Just take a look at these findings. They will likely **shock** you. After just 17 hours without sleep, you are as alert as someone who is almost legally drunk! After 24 hours without sleep, you are as alert as someone who has had several alcoholic drinks. But you don't even need to go to these extremes to get this effect. It can also come from **regularly** missing just a couple of hours of sleep a night. For example, sleeping only six hours a night for ten nights straight will have the same effect on your brain as not sleeping for 24 hours. What's more, you can't undo this effect by getting just one good night's sleep. It takes three nights of **complete** rest to get back to normal.

« lack of sleep

« alcoholic drinks

3   In short, if you really want to perform at your best, you need to **make time** for sleep. Between seven and nine hours a night is ideal. Get this amount of rest and you will be amazed at how much clearer your mind is.

## Q UESTIONS

_____1. **What does "it" mean in the first paragraph?**
   (A) Cancer.
   (B) Hurting your health.
   (C) Your brain.
   (D) Getting too little sleep.

_____2. **Which of these people is "shocked"?**
   (A)        (B)        (C)        (D)

_____3. **Which of these has the opposite meaning of "regularly" in the second paragraph?**
   (A) Easily.   (B) Seldom.   (C) Often.   (D) Poorly.

_____4. **What is another word for "complete" in the second paragraph?**
   (A) Full.   (B) Lazy.   (C) Strange.   (D) Warm.

_____5. **What does the phrase "make time" mean in the final paragraph?**
   (A) To write down the time that something begins.
   (B) To do something in a shorter time than usual.
   (C) To keep enough time free to do something.
   (D) To spend time doing useless things.

# 29 Now or After Lunch?

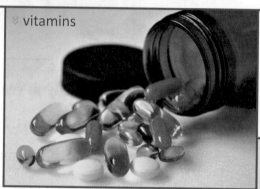
⌄ vitamins

**1** You know that taking vitamins is good for you, but did you also know that when and how you take them is important? Here are the best times and ways to take different kinds of vitamins.

**2** → Vitamins B and C are water soluble. It means they break down in water to be **absorbed** by the body. They are best taken before you eat in the morning or between meals. Vitamin C also helps your body to absorb iron, so they should be taken together.

**3** → Some vitamins are fat soluble, so they need fat to **dissolve**. These include vitamins A, D, E, and K. They should be taken with food or snacks which contain fat, such as nuts, eggs, and cheese.

**4** → Multivitamins contain both water soluble and fat soluble vitamins, so they should be taken with food as well. This allows the fat soluble vitamins to break down and only **slightly** affects the absorption of the water soluble ones.

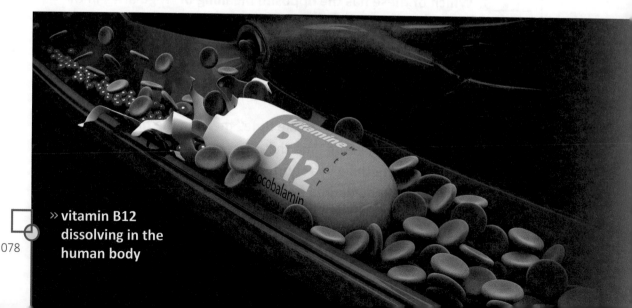
» vitamin B12
dissolving in the
human body

5 → Magnesium is not a vitamin, but it is very important for your health. It can be taken at any time of day, although some people experience stomach **trouble** when they take it without food.

6 In short, the time of day when you take vitamins is not as important as whether you take them with or without food. Taking water soluble vitamins **on an empty stomach** and fat soluble vitamins with meals allows your body to process them most effectively and efficiently.

« stomach trouble

# **Q** UESTIONS

_____1. **Which word has the opposite meaning of "absorbed"?**
(A) Found.　(B) Bought.　(C) Rejected.　(D) Eaten.

_____2. **What does it mean when something "dissolves"?**
(A) It breaks down.　　(B) It makes you stronger.
(C) It gets dirty.　　(D) It cannot be used.

_____3. **Which word has the opposite meaning of "slightly"?**
(A) Quickly.　(B) Slowly.　(C) Quietly.　(D) Greatly.

_____4. **What is another word for "trouble" as it is used in the passage?**
(A) Crime.　(B) Difficulty.　(C) Pain.　(D) Appetite.

_____5. **What does it mean to take something "on an empty stomach"?**
(A) You eat before you take it.
(B) You don't eat before you take it.
(C) You exercise before you take it.
(D) You take it when you are full.

# 30 A Master of Smells

⩔ A nose should be able to identify different smells.

**1** In any perfume company, the most important person is most certainly the nose. Though it sounds more like a body part than a job title, the "nose" is the person who *creates* a company's famous scents. In the same way that an artist creates a painting by **combining** different colors, a nose creates perfumes by combining different smells.

**2** Noses need to have a lot of knowledge, as well as an excellent sense of smell. They must be able to **identify** thousands of different smells and understand how they work together. They must also know how smells change over time and how they make people feel. When

⩔ perfumes

« A nose's job is to make perfumes.

a company has an idea for a new perfume, they will give their nose a description of both the scent and the feelings they want it to inspire in people. A good nose will be able to choose the ingredients that, mixed together, will **bring this idea to life**.

3   Becoming a nose is **no easy task**. Today, most noses need to have advanced degrees in chemistry before they even start training in the perfume business. However, with hard work comes great rewards. If a nose does end up creating a truly great perfume, it will be sold to millions of people around the world **for years to come**.

# Q UESTIONS

_____ 1. **What is another word for "combining" in the first paragraph?**
   (A) Writing.      (B) Mixing.      (C) Burning.      (D) Laughing.

_____ 2. **What does it mean if you are able to "identify" something?**
   (A) You can tell what it is.        (B) You can take it apart.
   (C) You can put it together.        (D) You can make it look new.

_____ 3. **What does it mean to "bring something to life"?**
   (A) Make something disappear.    (B) Make something popular.
   (C) Make something simpler.      (D) Make something real.

_____ 4. **What does it mean if something is "no easy task"?**
   (A) It is cheap.                 (B) It is difficult.
   (C) It is common.                (D) It is boring.

_____ 5. **Which of these has the opposite meaning to "for years to come"?**
   (A) For many people.             (B) For a long time.
   (C) For just a few people.       (D) For a short time.

# UNIT

# 3

# Study Strategies

**3-1**

**Visual Material**

**3-2**

**Reference Sources**

Visual material like charts and graphs, and reference sources like indexes and dictionaries, all provide important information. What's more, they help you understand complicated information more quickly than you can by reading. In this unit, you will learn to use them to gather information.

# 31 Water Power!

**1**    When you hear the term "renewable energy," what comes to mind? Wind power? Solar? These are the kinds of renewable energy people usually know about, likely because they are the most visible. Giant wind turbines and roofs covered in solar panels are, after all, hard to miss! But there is another type of renewable energy that often goes unnoticed: hydropower—energy created by water.

**2**    Hydropower is a great way to create energy without hurting the planet. A hydropower station usually has a large source of water nearby. The station can control how much energy it creates by changing the flow of water from the source. If a lot of energy is suddenly needed, it simply lets out more water. Right now, around 7% of the world's electricity is created by water—that is more than solar and wind combined! In fact, some countries are almost *completely* powered by water. Take a look at the map on the next page. It shows the countries of the world along with what share (%) of each one's electricity was created with water in the year 2020.

## Q UESTIONS

_____1. **What share of Australia's electricity was created through hydropower in 2020?**
 (A) Between 1% and 20%.　　　(B) Between 21% and 40%.
 (C) Between 41% and 60%.　　　(D) Between 61% and 80%.

_____2. **Which of the following countries generated more than 80% of its electricity through hydropower in 2020?**
 (A) The United States. (B) Russia.　(C) Greenland.　(D) Brazil.

_____3. **In which country was the share of electricity created by hydropower in 2020 either zero or not known?**
 (A) Saudi Arabia.　　　(B) Japan.　(C) New Zealand. (D) The United Kingdom.

≪ hydropower station    » solar panels

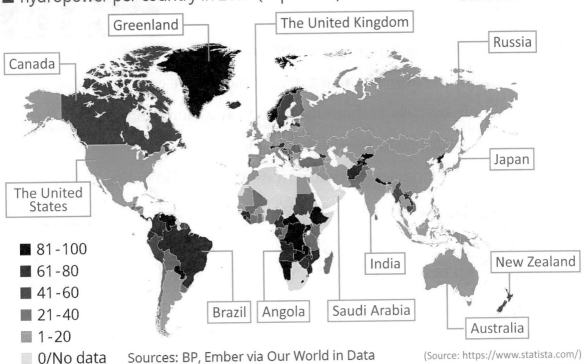

# How Water Powers the World

Share of electricity generated through
hydropower per country in 2020 (in percent)

statista

Greenland
The United Kingdom
Russia
Canada
Japan
The United States

81 - 100
61 - 80
41 - 60
21 - 40
1 - 20
0/No data

India
New Zealand
Brazil    Angola    Saudi Arabia
Australia

Sources: BP, Ember via Our World in Data    (Source: https://www.statista.com/)

_____ 4. Which of these is TRUE about India?

(A) In 2020, more than 40% of its electricity was created by hydropower.

(B) In 2020, a larger share (%) of its electricity was created by hydropower than Brazil.

(C) It is not known what share (%) of its electricity was created by hydropower in 2020.

(D) In 2020, a smaller share (%) of its electricity was created by hydropower than Canada.

_____ 5. What share of Angola's electricity was created through hydropower in 2020?

(A) Zero (or no data).    (B) Between 1% and 20%.

(C) Between 21% and 40%.    (D) Between 61% and 80%.

# 32 A New Home During COVID-19

**1** In 2019, animal shelters in the United States took in almost 350,000 animals. In the same year, only around 54% of animals in shelters were adopted. Then COVID-19 struck the world. And it had a *big* effect on these numbers.

⌃ shelter animals

**2** From 2019 to 2021, the number of animals entering shelters dropped to just over 260,000. We can only guess why this fell so much. Perhaps having to stay at home during COVID-19 made people love their pets more.

**3** Further, a far higher portion of those animals that did end up in shelters were adopted. The line graph on the next page shows these numbers. (A line graph shows numbers as dots joined by a line. This makes it easy to see how they rise and fall over time.) Of course, some people adopt animals from shelters without thinking deeply. And they take them back to the shelters soon after. Let's hope, though, that those pets adopted during COVID-19 truly have found their forever homes.

» Due to COVID-19, many people adopted pets from shelters.

# % of Shelter Animals That Were Adopted (US)

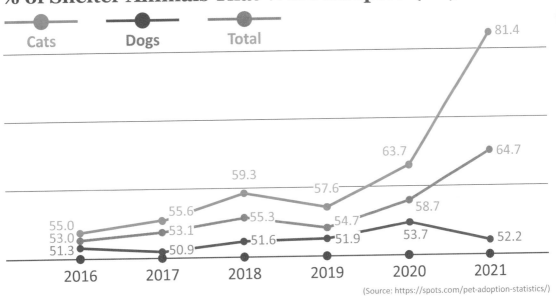

(Source: https://spots.com/pet-adoption-statistics/)

## QUESTIONS

_____1. In the first sentence, the writer says that in 2019, "around 54%" of animals in shelters were adopted. What is the true number according to the graph?
   (A) 54.9%    (B) 54.1%    (C) 54.7%    (D) 54.3%

_____2. According to the graph, what percentage (%) of shelter animals were adopted in the year 2018?
   (A) 51.6%    (B) 55.3%    (C) 59.3%    (D) 53.1%

_____3. Look at the graph. Which of the following describes something that happened in US shelters from 2018 to 2019?
   (A) The percentage (%) of animals that were adopted stayed the same.
   (B) The percentage (%) of dogs that were adopted fell.
   (C) The percentage (%) of cats that were adopted fell.
   (D) The percentage (%) of animals that were adopted grew.

_____4. According to the graph, in which year did 50.9% of shelter dogs get adopted?
   (A) 2017.    (B) 2016.    (C) 2020.    (D) 2019.

_____5. During which time did the percentage (%) of shelter cats that were adopted grow by less than 1%?
   (A) From 2017 to 2018.    (B) From 2020 to 2021.
   (C) From 2019 to 2020.    (D) From 2016 to 2017.

» In many countries, birth rates are falling, and elderly people are making up a larger percentage of the population.

# 33 The World's Oldest Countries

**1**     Two hundred years ago, the average person could expect to live only to around 40 years old. Today, that number has grown to 72.98 years. And in some countries, people can expect to live to more than 80! At the same time, the number of children being born in many countries is falling each year. This means that in some countries, elderly people (that is, people aged 65 and over) are making up a greater and greater part of the population. These countries, known as "aging societies," have a big challenge on their hands. They have to find ways of taking care of more and more old people while fewer and fewer young people contribute to the economy.

**2**     The bar chart on the next page shows some of the world's aging societies. A bar chart shows numbers as rectangles or "bars" of different lengths. The larger the number, the longer the bar. In the chart on the next page, countries are listed down the left-hand side. The percentage of each country's population aged 65 and over is shown as a bar next to the name.

## QUESTIONS

_____ 1. **According to the chart, in which country do elderly people make up 22.5% of the population?**
   (A) Monaco.  (B) Japan.     (C) Italy.      (D) Greece.

_____ 2. **According to the chart, how much of Italy's population is aged 65 and over?**
   (A) 23.7%     (B) 29.8%      (C) 36.0%     (D) 22.6%

_____ 3. **According to the chart, which of the following countries has the highest percentage of elderly people?**
   (A) Finland.  (B) Portugal.  (C) Japan.     (D) Saint Helena.

☆ People live much longer today than they did 200 years ago.

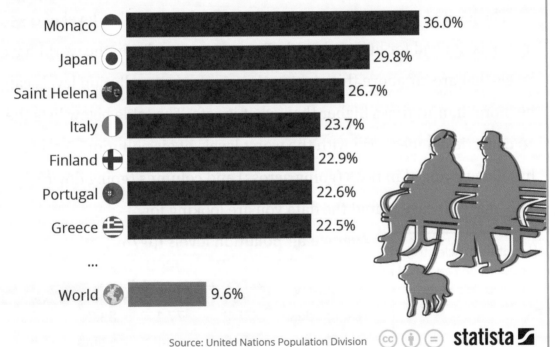

# The World's Aging Societies
Estimated share of population aged 65+ in 2021 by country/area

- Monaco — 36.0%
- Japan — 29.8%
- Saint Helena — 26.7%
- Italy — 23.7%
- Finland — 22.9%
- Portugal — 22.6%
- Greece — 22.5%
- ...
- World — 9.6%

Source: United Nations Population Division

statista

(Source: https://www.statista.com/)

_____4. **Which of the following statements is NOT true, according to the chart?**
(A) In Monaco, elderly people make up 36% of the population.
(B) In Finland, elderly people make up 22.9% of the population.
(C) Saint Helena has a lower percentage of elderly people than Italy.
(D) Greece has a lower percentage of elderly people than Portugal.

_____5. **What percentage of all the people in the world are aged 65 and over, according to the chart?**
(A) 9.6%  (B) 10.1%  (C) 4.5%  (D) 0.4%

» Cars release lots of particles into the air.

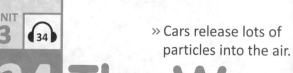

# 34 The Worst Places to Breathe

**1** In our modern world, air pollution is a big problem. Cars, scooters, trucks, and buses release huge amounts of particles into the air. So does burning coal, oil, and wood. These particles are so tiny that thousands of them could fit into a period at the end of this sentence. This makes them very harmful as they can travel deep into your lungs. And breathing in too many too often can cause lots of serious health problems.

**2** The level of pollution in the air is measured in μg/m³. A level of 0–5 μg/m³ is not bad for human health. But most countries in the world have levels that are far above this. And in the worst cases, pollution levels can be more than 10 times higher than what is safe. The table below lists the 10 countries in the world with the worst levels of air pollution. A table has data arranged in rows (going across) and columns (going down). This makes it easy to find the data you are looking for.

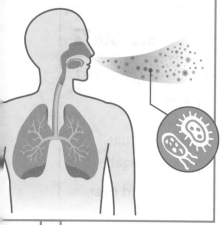

⌄ Harmful particles from air pollution can travel into people's lungs.

**Average air pollution levels (μg/m³) in the 10 most polluted countries, 2018–2021**

| Country | 2021 | 2020 | 2019 | 2018 |
|---|---|---|---|---|
| Bangladesh | 76.9 | 77.1 | 83.3 | 97.1 |
| Chad | 75.9 | no data | no data | no data |
| Pakistan | 66.8 | 59 | 65.8 | 74.3 |
| Tajikistan | 59.4 | 30.9 | no data | no data |
| India | 58.1 | 51.9 | 58.1 | 72.5 |
| Oman | 53.9 | 44.4 | no data | no data |
| Kyrgyzstan | 50.8 | 43.5 | 33.2 | no data |
| Bahrain | 49.8 | 39.7 | 46.8 | 59.8 |
| Iraq | 49.7 | no data | no data | no data |
| Nepal | 46 | 39.2 | 44.5 | 54.1 |

# Q UESTIONS

_____1. According to the table, which country had the eighth highest level of air pollution in 2021?

(A) Iraq.  (B) Nepal.  (C) Chad.  (D) Bahrain.

_____2. According to the table, what was the average air pollution level in India in 2020?

(A) $51.9 \ \mu g/m^3$
(C) $72.5 \ \mu g/m^3$
(B) $58.1 \ \mu g/m^3$
(D) $75.9 \ \mu g/m^3$

_____3. According to the table, in which years was the air pollution level in Pakistan between 60 and 70 $\mu g/m^3$?

(A) 2020 and 2019.
(C) 2021 and 2019.
(B) 2019 and 2018.
(D) 2021 and 2018.

_____4. Which of the following is TRUE according to the table?

(A) In 2021, Bangladesh had the second highest level of air pollution in the world.
(B) In 2020, India had a higher level of air pollution than Pakistan.
(C) In Bahrain, the level of air pollution fell from 2018 to 2019.
(D) In Nepal, the level of air pollution fell from 2020 to 2021.

_____5. Look at the table. Which of the following statements can we NOT say is either true or false?

(A) In Kyrgyzstan, the air pollution level in 2020 was higher than in 2019.
(B) In Oman, the air pollution level in 2019 was lower than in 2020.
(C) In Nepal, the air pollution level in 2018 was $54.1 \ \mu g/m^3$.
(D) In 2021, the air pollution in Iraq was lower than Bahrain.

# 35 Taiwan's Biggest Killer

**1** Death is not a nice thing to think about. However, knowing some of the statistics around death can help you make better choices about your health. Every year, Taiwan's Ministry of Health and Welfare releases the number of deaths in Taiwan for the previous year. In 2021, there were more than 184,172 deaths in Taiwan, and the disease that caused the most deaths by far was cancer, which took 51,656 lives. In fact, cancer has been the leading cause of death in Taiwan since the 1980s.

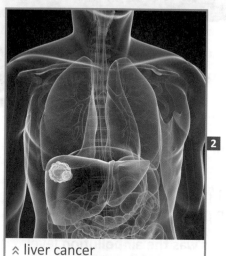

⌃ liver cancer

⌃ colon cancer

**2** Take a look at the pie chart on the next page. It shows different types of cancer and the number of deaths caused by each one of them in Taiwan in 2021. A pie chart represents the relationship between parts and the whole. The whole is the circle, or "pie" (in this case, it's Taiwan's 51,656 deaths from cancer).

## Q UESTIONS

_____1. **According to the pie chart, which type of cancer caused 15.4% of cancer-related deaths in Taiwan in 2021?**
(A) Oral cancer.  (B) Liver cancer.  (C) Colon cancer.  (D) Stomach cancer.

_____2. **Which of these statements is TRUE, based on the pie chart?**
(A) Breast cancer caused 12.9% of cancer-related deaths in Taiwan in 2021.
(B) Ovarian cancer caused 6.6% of cancer-related deaths in Taiwan in 2021.
(C) Prostate cancer caused 5.6% of cancer-related deaths in Taiwan in 2021.
(D) Pancreatic cancer caused 5.1% of cancer-related deaths in Taiwan in 2021.

⥥ lung cancer

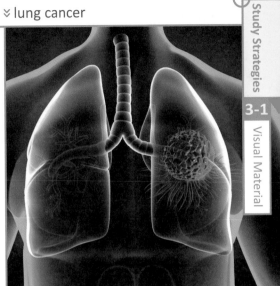

The parts are the "slices" of the pie. As you can see, the type of cancer that killed the most people was lung cancer. And as most people are aware by now, one of the main causes of lung cancer is smoking cigarettes. So by avoiding this harmful habit, you can also lower your chances of becoming a cancer statistic.

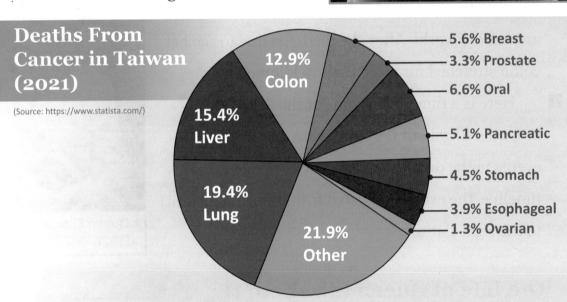

**Deaths From Cancer in Taiwan (2021)**

(Source: https://www.statista.com/)

- 12.9% Colon
- 15.4% Liver
- 19.4% Lung
- 21.9% Other
- 5.6% Breast
- 3.3% Prostate
- 6.6% Oral
- 5.1% Pancreatic
- 4.5% Stomach
- 3.9% Esophageal
- 1.3% Ovarian

_____3. Together, breast, stomach, and pancreatic cancer caused what share of cancer-related deaths in Taiwan in 2021?

(A) 15.2%   (B) 13.2%   (C) 11.4%  (D) 14.6%

_____4. According to the chart, which of the following caused a greater share of deaths than oral cancer in Taiwan in 2021?

(A) Prostate cancer.　　(B) Colon cancer.
(C) Ovarian cancer.　　(D) Stomach cancer.

_____5. Which of the following types of cancer caused the fewest deaths in Taiwan in 2021?

(A) Lung cancer.　　(B) Breast cancer.
(C) Pancreatic cancer.　　(D) Esophageal cancer.

# 36 A Life on the Throne

**1** On September 8, 2022, the world heard some very sad news. Elizabeth II, Queen of the United Kingdom, had died at the age of 96. She ruled for over 70 years, a length of time that made her the second-longest reigning monarch in history. She was a very popular ruler, and she was loved not only by her subjects in the UK but also by millions more around the world. After she died, the line to see her coffin stretched for more than 16 kilometers!

**2** Here is a timeline of some of the key events in Queen Elizabeth II's long life. A timeline lists events in the order in which they happened. In this timeline, the events are listed from the left (earliest) to the right (latest).

⌃ Queen Elizabeth II
(1926–2022)

## The Life of Queen Elizabeth II

**1926**
Elizabeth Alexandra Mary Windsor is born.

**1940**
Makes her first public speech over the radio to comfort the children affected by World War II.

**1947**
Marries Prince Phillip.

**1948**
Gives birth to her first child, Charles.

**1952**
Becomes Queen Elizabeth II after the death of her father, King George VI.

« People are paying their respects at Buckingham Palace after the death of Queen Elizabeth II, September 9, 2022.

# Q UESTIONS

_____1. **Which of these events in Elizabeth II's life happened first?**
(A) She gave birth to her first child.
(B) She married Prince Phillip.
(C) She became Queen.
(D) She opened the London Olympics.

_____2. **In what year did Elizabeth II marry Prince Philip?**
(A) 1948  (B) 1926  (C) 1940  (D) 1947

_____3. **Which of these events happened in 2021?**
(A) Elizabeth II celebrated 25 years on the throne.
(B) Elizabeth II became Queen.
(C) Elizabeth II's husband, Philip, died.
(D) Elizabeth II and her husband celebrated 70 years of marriage.

_____4. **According to the timeline, in which two years did Elizabeth give important speeches to the nation?**
(A) 1940 and 2020.  (B) 1960 and 1977.
(C) 2002 and 2021.  (D) 1964 and 2022.

_____5. **Which of these events happened after 1960?**
(A) Elizabeth II's father died.
(B) Elizabeth II gave birth to her first child.
(C) Elizabeth II made her first public speech.
(D) Elizabeth II celebrated 25 years on the throne.

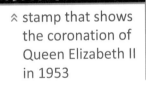

THE CORONATION 1953

⌃ stamp that shows the coronation of Queen Elizabeth II in 1953

**1977**
Celebrates 25 years on the throne.

**2020**
COVID-19 hits the UK. Makes an encouraging speech to the nation.

**2022**
Celebrates 70 years on the throne. Dies of old age aged 96 on September 8.

**2012**
Opens the London Olympics.

**2021**
Her husband, Phillip, dies peacefully aged 99.

# 37 Studying the Mind

**1**      How does the human mind work? Why do we behave the way we do? These are the questions the science of psychology hopes to answer.

**2**      Psychology is a fairly "young" science. It only really got going around 150 years ago. But still, during that time, a *lot* has been discovered. In any library or bookstore you will find shelf after shelf of books about the subject. For beginners, though, these books can be difficult to understand. Just like any science, psychology uses lots of special words and phrases. So, when reading a psychology book, it can be helpful to have a glossary on hand.

**3**      A glossary is a kind of short dictionary. It contains words related to a specific subject. Just like in a dictionary, the words are listed from A to Z. On the next page is the first section of a psychology glossary.

⌄ adrenalin

ADRENALIN

## Q UESTIONS

_____1. **According to the glossary, which of the following words means "the fear of being in busy public places"?**
(A) Altruism.      (B) Amnesia.      (C) Antidepressant. (D) Agoraphobia.

_____2. **According to the glossary, what does the word "adolescence" mean?**
(A) Feeling nervous or worried.
(B) When someone loses their ability to use language.
(C) Caring about the needs of others even when there is no reward.
(D) The time in someone's life between being a child and being an adult.

_____3. **Which of the following words would you most likely find in the second section of the glossary?**
(A) Depression.      (B) Biases.      (C) Euphoria.      (D) Illusions.

# Glossary

## A

**addiction:** not being able to stop doing something, especially something that is bad for your health

**adolescence:** the time in someone's life between being a child and being an adult

**adrenalin:** a chemical that your body releases when you feel excited or afraid, making your heart beat faster

**agoraphobia:** the fear of being in busy public places

**altruism:** caring about the needs of others even when there is no reward

**amnesia:** when someone loses all or part of their memory

**antidepressant:** a medicine used to make a person feel less sad

**anxiety:** feeling nervous or worried

**aphasia:** when someone loses their ability to use language

**automatic behavior:** an action that is done without thinking

˅ aphasia

_____ 4. The word "anchoring" is not in this glossary, but if it were, where would you find it?
   (A) Between "anxiety" and "aphasia."
   (B) Between "amnesia" and "antidepressant."
   (C) Between "addiction" and "adolescence."
   (D) Between "adrenalin" and "agoraphobia."

_____ 5. According to the glossary, what is "automatic behavior"?
   (A) An action that is done without thinking.
   (B) A medicine used to make a person feel less sad.
   (C) A chemical that your body releases when you feel excited or afraid.
   (D) Not being able to stop doing something, especially something that is bad for your health.

# 38 Time Control!

**1**     Do you often find yourself running out of time? Maybe you wanted to play video games after school, but you took too long finishing your homework. Maybe you wanted to eat breakfast, but you took too long getting your school bag ready. If these things happen to you, then you probably need to learn how to manage your time better!

**2**     There are lots of books out there that can teach you how to do this. *Time Control* by Tina Zhang, is one example. On the next page is the table of contents from that book. A table of contents lists the chapters and sections that are in a book, along with their page numbers. By looking at a book's table of contents, you can get a better idea of the kind of information that is in the book.

⌃ time management

## Q UESTIONS

⌃ putting your phone away

_____1. **On which page of the book *Time Control* would you find a chapter on calendars?**

    (A) 21.     (B) 30.     (C) 20.     (D) 39.

_____2. **What is chapter 8 of the book about?**

    (A) The A-B-C method.     (B) Putting your phone away.

    (C) Setting your goals.     (D) To-do lists.

# Contents

_____ **3. In which part of the book would you find information about staying focused?**

  (A) Part 1.     (B) Part 2.     (C) Part 3.     (D) Part 4.

_____ **4. In which chapter would you find information about the differences between "important" things and "urgent" things?**

  (A) Chapter 6.   (B) Chapter 5.   (C) Chapter 9.   (D) Chapter 2.

_____ **5. How long is Chapter 9 in this book?**

  (A) Eleven pages. (B) One page.   (C) Twenty pages. (D) Ninety-five pages.

# 39 Get Your Fingers Green!

**1**    Are you looking for a new hobby—one that is both fun and fulfilling? Then why not try gardening? Taking care of plants and watching them grow is a really great feeling. And you don't need a big piece of land to get started either. If you have a balcony or even just a windowsill—anywhere that gets lots of light—you can garden! You can grow flowers, herbs, vegetables, fruit—anything you like! In your garden, you are the boss!

**2**    If you are new to gardening, it is a good idea to get a beginner's guide. These guides have information on many different types of plants. They also have tips and tricks for making your plants grow well. If you want to learn about a particular topic (e.g., "tomatoes" or "soil"), take a look at the index at the back. The index is a list from A to Z of all the things covered in the book, along with the pages on which they were mentioned. It makes finding specific information very easy.

**3**    On the next page, for example, is a section of the index from the book *Fresh Green Fingers: A Guide for First-Time Gardeners.*

## Q UESTIONS

_____1. **Aphids are bugs that cause damage to many garden plants. On which page of the book would you find information about them?**
(A) 159.          (B) 100.          (C) 72.          (D) 157.

_____2. **How many pages in the book are there about plants that attract butterflies?**
(A) Two.          (B) Three.          (C) One.          (D) Four.

_____3. **What would you find information about on page 51?**
(A) How to make compost.          (B) Watering container gardens.
(C) Buying fertilizer.          (D) Drought.

⌃ windowsill

⌃ compost

# INDEX

**A**

annuals

buying, 49

caring for, 113–114

cold-weather, 100

hot-weather

shade, 112

sun, 111

planting, 99

aphids, 159

**B**

bagworms, 106

blackspot, 105

brown patches, 85

bulbs, flowering, 135–140

butterfly-attracting plants, 130-132

**C**

cabbage white butterfly, 160

compost

how to make, 71

ingredients, 72

problems, 72

container gardens

caring for, 176

deadheading, 177

fertilizing, 175

planting, 171–174, 178

trees, 177

watering, 175

containers

buying, 59

in small spaces, 170

**D**

deadheading

annuals, 113

container gardens, 177

perennials, 112

decomposing, *see compost*

double digging, 128

drought, 157

**E**

edging, 163

evergreens, 94

**F**

fertilizer

buying, 51

non-organic, 62

organic, 63

fertilizing

annuals, 112

container gardens, 175

flowering plants

annuals

caring for, 113–114

choosing, 109

---

_____ **4. Where would an entry for "bamboo" come in this index?**

(A) Before "bagworms."

(B) Between "blackspot" and "brown patches."

(C) Between "brown patches" and "bulbs, flowering."

(D) Between "bagworms" and "blackspot."

_____ **5. "Deadheading" means cutting dead flowers from plants in order to keep them growing. On which pages of the book would you find information about it?**

(A) 128 and 157.　　(B) 175 and 177.

(C) 112, 113, and 177.　　(D) 171, 174, and 178.

» a perfect angle for taking a selfie

# 40 Hey, Me. Say Cheese!

45°

» selfie stick

**1**     Taking "selfies," or pictures of yourself with your phone, can be lots of fun. But it can be hard to get a really great shot. There are lots of guides on the Internet about how to take better selfies. To find a guide, do a web search. When you type a word or phrase into a search engine and press enter, you'll get a list of results. Each result contains a title, a web address, and a short extract of what is on the web page. Here are some results that can come up after you type "selfie."

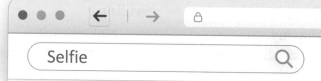

Selfie     🔍

www.what-words-mean.com/selfie

**What does "Selfie" mean? – What Words Mean**

A selfie is a photo of a person taken by that person. Selfies are often taken with a phone or a digital camera . . . .

www.tv-guide.org/shows/S/selfie

**Selfie (TV show) – TV Guide**

*Selfie* is the title of a US comedy show. It began in 2014 and stars Karen Gillan and John Cho . . . .

www.culturemagazine.com/internet/may2014/how-selfies

**Everyone Is Taking Selfies. Is That a Good Thing? – Culture Magazine**

May 12, 2014, by Joan Snow – Everyone from kids to grandparents is taking selfies these days. But is this new habit a good thing or a bad thing? . . . .

⌃ taking a selfie

www.goodbuys.com.tw/phones/5TsTPN76

**Selfie Stick, 1 Meter Long, Very Strong, $9.99 . . . .**

A 1-meter-long selfie stick made of strong metal. It can be made longer or shorter to easily fit in your bag. Buy now for just $9.99 . . . .

www.teenlife.net/blog/how-to-take-a-selfie

**How to Take a Selfie: 8 Tips to Take a Better Pic of Yourself**

Jun. 3, 2021 – Contents: 1. Angle 2. Eyes 3. Light 4. Smile 5. Flash 6. View 7. Find Your Good Side 8. Practice.

# **Q** UESTIONS

_____ 1. **Which website should you visit to get tips on how to take a better selfie?**
(A) www.teenlife.net
(B) www.culturemagazine.com
(C) www.tv-guide.org
(D) www.what-words-mean.com

_____ 2. **If you visited www.goodbuys.com, what would you find?**
(A) Information about a TV show named "Selfie."
(B) Information about a selfie stick that is for sale.
(C) An article about how selfies became so popular.
(D) Information about what the word "selfie" means.

_____ 3. **Who are Karen Gillan and John Cho?**
(A) People who bought a selfie stick.
(B) Writers for Culture Magazine.
(C) The people who invented the word "selfie."
(D) Actors in the TV show "Selfie."

_____ 4. **Which of these is TRUE about the article "Everyone Is Taking Selfies. Is That a Good Thing?"**
(A) It was published on June 3, 2021.
(B) It was published in Teen Life magazine.
(C) It ends by saying that taking selfies is a bad thing.
(D) It was written by Joan Snow.

_____ 5. **Which of these is NOT mentioned in the article on how to take a better selfie?**
(A) Flash.     (B) Eyes.
(C) Clothes.   (D) Smile.

# UNIT
# 4

# Final Review

**4-1**

Review: Reading Skills

**4-2**

Review: Word Study

**4-3**

Review: Visual Material

**4-4**

Review: Reference Sources

In this unit, you will review what you have learned. From these comprehensive questions, you can examine how well you have absorbed the ideas and material in this book.

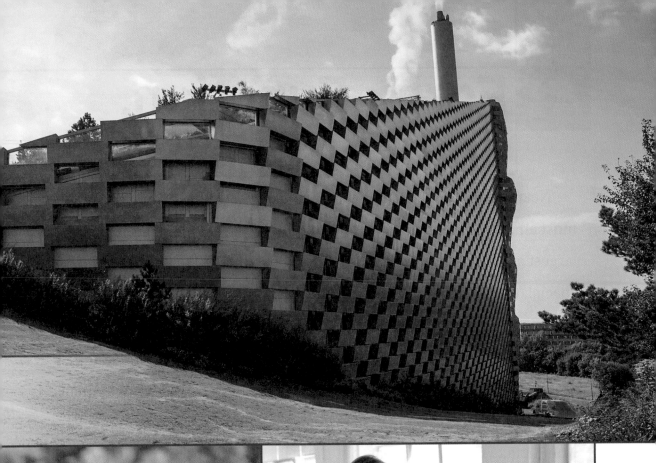

# 41 Form, Function, and Fun

1    Near the center of Copenhagen, Denmark's capital, is one of the most amazing buildings ever designed. Known as CopenHill, it is the largest and tallest building in the city, but that is not what makes it so special. CopenHill is as unique on the inside as it is on the outside.

2    Opened in 2019, CopenHill is the world's cleanest waste-to-energy plant. Every year it burns 440,000 tons of trash, turning it into enough clean energy to power and heat 100,000 local homes. And it does all of this without releasing any poisons into the atmosphere. That in itself would make CopenHill great, but there is still more. This is a building you can actually play with.

3    Copenhill's roof is an outdoor activity center that people can enjoy. It offers hiking trails, playgrounds, exercise areas, and great views of the city. The building's walls can even be climbed. Topping it all off is a 450-meter artificial ski slope, the very first ski slope in Denmark. So not only does CopenHill take care of garbage and provide power, but it is also an important recreation spot.

» CopenHill

≪ the climbing wall of CopenHill

≪ CopenHill provides exercise areas for people.

**4**     CopenHill was designed by BIG, a company run by Copenhagen-born architect Bjarke Ingels. In 2011, the group won a contest to create a waste-to-energy plant for the city and decided to make something that would do much more. As Ingels says, "A sustainable city is not only better for the environment—it is also more enjoyable for the lives of its citizens."

## **Q** UESTIONS

_____ 1. **What is the main idea of this article?**
  (A) Bjarke Ingels is a great architect.
  (B) CopenHill is a place where many things happen.
  (C) CopenHill is the largest building in Copenhagen.
  (D) People in Denmark really enjoy exercising.

_____ 2. **Which of the following is NOT mentioned as something people can do at CopenHill?**
  (A) Go hiking.        (B) Go climbing.
  (C) Look at Copenhagen.    (D) Play basketball.

_____ 3. **Why did BIG design CopenHill?**
  (A) Because many skiers work at BIG.
  (B) Because Copenhagen had no recreation spots.
  (C) Because no one else wanted to do it.
  (D) Because it won a contest.

_____ 4. **How does the writer seem to feel about CopenHill?**
  (A) Excited.    (B) Bored.    (C) Angry.     (D) Uncomfortable.

_____ 5. **What can we guess from the third paragraph?**
  (A) Most of the people at CopenHill are children.
  (B) CopenHill is only open in the winter.
  (C) Skiing isn't very popular in Denmark.
  (D) People can take their garbage to this building.

# 42 The Doctor Who Became a God

⌄ Asclepius, Greek god of medicine

**1**      Have you ever wondered why the logo for the World Health Association features a snake wrapped round a stick? What on earth does a snake and a stick have to do with medicine? In fact, this symbol is linked to the ancient Greek god of medicine, Asclepius.

**2**      The story goes that Asclepius was born to a mortal woman named Koronis and the god Apollo. As a boy, Asclepius did not have an ordinary education. His father sent him to the centaur Chiron, a being who was half-horse, half-man. Chiron was known for his skills in medicine—skills which he passed on to his new student.

**3**      Asclepius turned out to be a great healer. He also began carrying a stick with a snake wrapped around it as his symbol, since the Greeks thought snakes had special healing powers. However, his talent turned out to be his downfall. He was so good at healing that people weren't dying like they were supposed to. So the god of the dead, Hades, complained about him to Zeus, the king of the gods. To bring balance back to the world, Zeus struck Asclepius dead with a lightning bolt. Of course, this made Apollo furious. So to make peace, Zeus agreed to make Asclepius a god, too.

**4**      In ancient Greece, temples to Asclepius became important centers of healing. People would travel to them from far and wide to find cures and to study the art of medicine. Today, many consider these healing centers—known as *Asclepieia*—to be the birthplace of modern medicine.

✦ sanctuary of Asclepius at Epidaurus, Greece

# Q UESTIONS

_____ 1. **Which of the following is shown on the logo of the World Health Association?**

(A)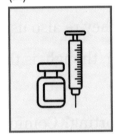

(B)

(C)

(D)

_____ 2. **What are the second and third paragraphs made up of?**

(A) A problem and a solution.    (B) A statement and examples.

(C) A series of events.    (D) A list of instructions.

_____ 3. **What caused Hades, the god of the dead, to complain to Zeus, the king of the gods?**

(A) Zeus agreeing to make Asclepius a god.

(B) Asclepius's amazing ability to stop people dying.

(C) Asclepius going to study with Chiron.

(D) Zeus striking down Asclepius with a lightning bolt.

_____ 4. **What is likely TRUE about Apollo?**

(A) He cared a lot about his son Asclepius.

(B) Asclepius was the only son he had.

(C) He was the son of Hades, god of the dead.

(D) He thought Chiron was a bad teacher.

_____ 5. **What is the writer's purpose in the last paragraph?**

(A) To show how smart the ancient Greeks were.

(B) To make the reader feel angry about Asclepius's death.

(C) To make the reader doubt the story of Asclepius.

(D) To show why the story of Asclepius is important to us today.

# 43 Food That Makes You Feel Good

**1**    What do you do to feel better when you are feeling down? Lots of people turn to certain dishes to make them feel good. These dishes are known as "comfort foods." Comfort foods may be different for everyone, but in general they share certain traits. They are often high in calories, and they tend to be either snack foods—like potato chips—or rich, home-cooked dishes—like bread-and-butter pudding. They're also usually sweet or salty rather than sour or bitter. The main thing, though, is that eating them gives you a warm, happy feeling inside.

**2**    But what is it that makes these foods so comforting? Comfort foods are usually linked with happy memories. Certain dishes (like maybe your grandma's chocolate cake) make you feel good because they remind you of people you love and happy times. What's more, our bodies love high-calorie foods because they give us a lot of energy. When we eat them, our brains reward us by sending out chemicals that make us feel good. Comfort foods are so powerful because they affect us both emotionally and physically.

**3**    Of course, there is nothing wrong with eating your favorite comfort food now and again. But because comfort foods are often high in calories, eating them every time you feel down probably isn't a good idea. The next time you are hungry for your comfort food, try making yourself feel better in a different way. This could be by going for a walk or taking a long bath. Limiting how often you eat your comfort food will stop it ever becoming a danger to your health.

« Comfort foods can make people feel happy.

↗ high-calorie foods

# Q UESTIONS

_____ 1. **Which of these does the writer give in the first paragraph?**

(A) Numbers.  (B) Examples.  (C) Directions.  (D) Advice.

_____ 2. **What is the main idea of the second paragraph?**

(A) Comfort foods can make people think of the people they love.

(B) Our bodies love high-calorie foods because they give us a lot of energy.

(C) Our brains reward us when we eat high-calorie foods.

(D) Comfort foods affect people both emotionally and physically.

_____ 3. **What is the writer's tone in the final paragraph?**

(A) Comic.  (B) Bitter.  (C) Cruel.  (D) Helpful.

_____ 4. **According to the article, which of the following is most likely to be someone's comfort food?**

(A) Fresh tomato salad.  (B) Bitter chocolate.

(C) Apple pie with cream.  (D) Lemons.

_____ 5. **Here are the results of a study in which people were asked when they felt like eating comfort foods the most.**

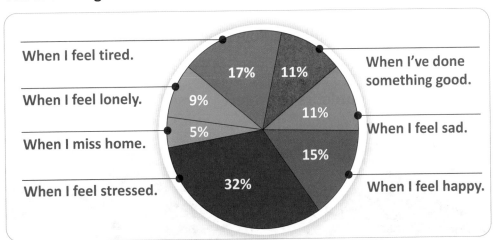

**What is the biggest cause of people wanting to eat comfort foods?**

(A) Feeling stressed.  (B) Feeling sad.

(C) Feeling lonely.  (D) Missing home.

# 44 Danger in the Garden

» leaves of water hemlock

1 Most people enjoy sitting in a garden full of beautiful flowers. But be careful: some of the most common plants around us are very dangerous.

2 One of these is water hemlock. This harmless-looking plant is a member of the carrot family, but do not eat it! Its stalk is full of a toxic liquid which can kill humans and other large animals. You can easily recognize it by its small, umbrella-shaped white flowers, and you should avoid it wherever you find it.

3 Then there's oleander, which is grown as a decorative flower in Taiwan and other places. Its red, white, pink, or yellow flowers are lovely and easy to care for. However, eating even a single leaf of the plant can be deadly. Ironically, oleander is used to make heart medicine, even though it can stop your heart forever.

4 Poison ivy is another plant to watch out for. Although it is not poisonous enough to kill you, touching it causes rashes, itching, and blisters. Poison ivy can reach over 30 meters in length. Cover your skin when you travel outdoors to protect yourself from this plant.

⌄ rhododendron flowers

« blisters

5　　Rhododendron flowers are popular in many places, including Taiwan. They bloom in April and May in red, purple, white, pink, yellow, and blue, as well as in different mixtures of these colors. The plant contains poison in all of its parts, however, and can cause vomiting, breathing trouble, and even coma.

6　　To put it simply, when you are around any of these plants, look but don't touch.

# Q UESTIONS

_____ 1. **What is the main idea of this article?**
(A) People should cover their skin when they go outdoors.
(B) It is nice to sit in a garden full of beautiful flowers.
(C) Oleander and rhododendron are popular in Taiwan.
(D) Many common and popular plants can be dangerous.

_____ 2. **Why is it bad to touch poison ivy?**
(A) You could die.　　　　　(B) You could get a rash.
(C) You could go into a coma.　　(D) You could have breathing trouble.

_____ 3. **How can we describe the writer's tone in this article?**
(A) Informative.　　(B) Angry.　　(C) Humorous.　　(D) Frightened.

_____ 4. **Which of the following is most likely a picture of water hemlock?**
(A)　　　　(B)　　　　(C)　　　　(D)

_____ 5. **How does the writer conclude the article?**
(A) With a personal story.　　(B) With a question.
(C) With a warning.　　　　(D) With a joke.

113

# 45 There to Listen and Help

← | →   🔒 https://www.oakwoodjuniorhigh.com/student-services/student-counseling

Home > Student Services > Student Counseling

**1** ## How Our Counselors Help

Our school counselors can help you with all kinds of problems, both **academic** and personal. Our counselors are there to listen to you and give you advice. They are not there to judge you but to help you. Some of the things our counselors can help you with are:

- Dealing with exam pressure
- Feeling nervous about high school
- Problems with a certain class or teacher
- Dealing with being bullied
- Dealing with problems at home (e.g., parents splitting up)
- Feeling pressure to smoke or take drugs

⌄ A school counselor helps students with many kinds of problems.

# Q UESTIONS

_____1. **What is another word for "drop by"?**
(A) Visit.   (B) Rest.   (C) Ignore.   (D) Catch.

_____2. **What does the word "academic" most likely mean?**
(A) Linked to sport.   (B) Linked to young children.
(C) Linked to cooking.   (D) Linked to school work.

_____3. **What is the opposite of "absent"?**
(A) Free.   (B) Lonely.   (C) Poor.   (D) Present.

_____4. **What is a "professional"?**
(A) A person who is doing something for the first time.
(B) A person with a lot of training and experience.
(C) A person who does not like listening to others.
(D) A person who has a lot of problems in their personal life.

≫ parents having a fight in front of their child

## 2 How Do I See a Counselor?

You can **drop by** the Counseling Office any time during opening hours and make an appointment to see a counselor. Don't worry if you have a class at your appointment time. The counselor will let your teacher know that you will be **absent** or late.

The Counseling Office is located in Building D, Room 4, and it is open from 8 a.m. to 5 p.m., Monday to Friday.

## 3 Meet Our Counselors

Currently, we have three counselors working at Oakwood Junior High School. Click on their names to learn more about them.

Ms. Polly Lee →    Mr. James Khan →    Ms. Selina Ramirez →

All our counselors are skilled **professionals** who have worked with young people for many years.

_____5. **If you click on "Ms. Polly Lee," you are shown the following information. What does "this" mean here?**

Ms. Polly Lee

Hi, students of Oakwood School. I'm Polly Lee. I have been working as a school counselor at Oakwood School for 10 years! Over this time, I've helped hundreds of students with their problems. I am especially good at helping students deal with exam pressure. If you need help with this in particular, you can ask for me specifically at the school counseling office. Being a student is hard, so don't be afraid to ask for help. After all, that's why I'm here!

(A) Being afraid to ask for help.     (B) Asking for Ms. Lee.
(C) Dealing with exam pressure.     (D) Being a student.

# 46 A New Table, Step by Step

## ASSEMBLY INSTRUCTIONS

1 Thank you for buying this table (item #: 23463566). To **assemble** the table, please follow the steps below carefully.

2 ### BEFORE YOU START

❶ Remove the plastic wrapping from the wooden table parts.

❷ Open the plastic bags that contain the hardware.

❸ Check the list below and make sure that everything is present before you start assembling the table.

❹ If any item is **missing**, please contact us using our customer service phone number or the form on our website.

❺ If everything is present, place the wooden parts on a clean floor and begin assembling.

| Hardware | Quantity |
|---|---|
| Washer | 8 |
| Bolt | 8 |
| Allen key | 1 |

| Table Parts | Quantity |
|---|---|
| Table top | 1 |
| Table leg | 4 |

## ▣ ASSEMBLY STEPS

**❶** Turn the table top upside down so that the table's surface is facing the floor.

**❷** Take one of the legs and place it, upside down, at one of the table's corners.

**❸** Line up the two holes in the top of the leg with the two holes in the table's corner.

**❹** Take a washer and push a bolt through it. Then screw the bolt, with the washer attached, into one of the two holes. (The **diagram** on the back of these instructions shows you clearly how to do this.)

**❺** Tighten the bolt with the Allen key.

**❻** Do the same again for the second hole. The leg should then be **secure**.

**❼** Repeat steps 2–6 for each leg.

**❽** Turn the table upright and place it in your desired spot.

## Q UESTIONS

_____1. **What does the word "assemble" most likely mean?**
   (A) To take something apart.
   (B) To put something together.
   (C) To make something more beautiful.
   (D) To make something easy to understand.

_____2. **Which word in the article is the opposite of "missing"?**
   (A) Wooden.    (B) Plastic.
   (C) Clean.      (D) Present.

_____3. **What is another word for "quantity" in the instructions?**
   (A) Cost.        (B) Weight.
   (C) Amount.    (D) Size.

_____4. **Which of these is another word for "diagram"?**
   (A) Picture.     (B) Game.
   (C) Song.        (D) Movie.

_____5. **What is another word for "secure"?**
   (A) Lost.         (B) Broken.
   (C) Firm.         (D) Dangerous.

# 47 It's Good to Be Wrong

⌃ Many people are afraid of making mistakes.

⌃ expert

How do you behave when you make a mistake? Do you scold yourself for being foolish and then hide your head in the sand? Many people **act this way** because they see mistakes as negative things. However, there are lots of reasons to see mistakes as being the complete opposite. In fact, if you handle making mistakes in the right way, you will experience many rewards.

Research has shown that if you make a mistake but then think about what you did wrong, new connections are made between nerve cells in the brain. Making mistakes can actually make your brain grow! To get this **result**, learn not to hide from your mistakes but rather face them and think deeply about them. Try to **figure out** what you did wrong and how you can avoid doing the same thing again.

## Q UESTIONS

3    Once you admit to yourself that it is fine to make mistakes, the door to many new and exciting learning opportunities will open to you. No one is an expert at anything in the beginning, but over time, and by making lots of mistakes, you can become one. Before you know it, you will have **a new string to your bow**. If you are always frozen by the fear of making mistakes, however, you will stay fixed and never grow as a person. Remember, you can do anything in life, but only if you are **willing** to get things wrong first!

_____1. **What does the writer mean by "act this way" in the first paragraph?**
  (A) Face your mistakes and then think deeply about them.
  (B) See mistakes as the opposite of negative things.
  (C) Admit to yourself that it is fine to make mistakes.
  (D) Scold yourself and then hide your head in the sand.

_____2. **Which of these is the opposite of "result" in the second paragraph?**
  (A) Cause.      (B) Answer.
  (C) Sign.       (D) Prize.

_____3. **What is another word for "figure out" in the second paragraph?**
  (A) Ignore.     (B) Understand.
  (C) Invent.     (D) Forget.

_____4. **What does "a new string to your bow" in the third paragraph most likely mean?**
  (A) An extra skill.
  (B) A long wait.
  (C) A hard test.
  (D) A new friend.

_____5. **What is another word for "willing" in the final sentence?**
  (A) Frightened.   (B) Surprised.
  (C) Prepared.     (D) Hated

« Making mistakes can help your brain grow.

# 48 "On Time" Around the World

**1**      What exactly does it mean to be "on time"? Are you still on time if you are five minutes late? Ten? A whole day? In fact, what counts as "on time" varies by culture. Here are some examples of what being on time means around the world.

**2**  **Mexico**

Being late in Mexico is really **no big deal**. Turning up 30 minutes late to a casual meeting or party is pretty much expected.

**3** **Japan**

Being late in Japan is seen as very rude behavior. In fact, most people will try to arrive 10 to 15 minutes early. If you are late, you'd better be ready to **apologize**!

**4** **Morocco**

Moroccans are famous for their relaxed **attitude** about time. By their standards, "on time" means anything from being 30 minutes to a *whole day* late!

## Q UESTIONS

_____ 1. **What does "no big deal" mean in the second paragraph?**
    (A) Not a serious problem.     (B) Not a good idea.
    (C) Not expensive.     (D) Not a long time.

_____ 2. **Which of these is another way to express the word "apologize" in the third paragraph?**
    (A) Be late.     (B) Stay home.
    (C) Give thanks.     (D) Say sorry.

« In Germany, traffic
delays aren't a good
excuse for being late.

» In Japan, people are
expected to apologize
if they are late.

**5** # Germany

Germans value being on time **a great deal**. There is *no excuse* for being late. You were stuck in traffic? Then you should have planned ahead and left early, shouldn't you?

**6** # Brazil

Delays are so expected in this country that it is seen as rude to turn up to a party at the scheduled time. Why? Because the host is certain to be running late themselves, and so will not be ready to **receive** you!

_____ 3. **What is another word for "attitude" in the fourth paragraph?**
   (A) Songs.   (B) Dishes.   (C) Feelings.   (D) Complaints.

_____ 4. **What is the opposite of "a great deal" in the fifth paragraph?**
   (A) Slowly.   (B) A little.   (C) Quickly.   (D) Very much.

_____ 5. **What does the word "receive" mean in the final paragraph?**
   (A) To work hard.        (B) To get a letter.
   (C) To hear some news.    (D) To welcome a guest.

# 49 Fur or Feathers?

1     At one time bats were believed to be strange-looking birds, but in fact the two animals are quite different.

2     Bats are mammals, so they give birth to live young. Their bodies are covered with fur, and they have jaws and sharp teeth. Their wings are actually large hands with thin skin that connects the fingers. The skin also connects their fingers to their legs. Since they hunt by night and cannot see very well, bats use a process called echolocation to locate their prey. In this process, bats give off sounds that bounce off their prey and come back to them, letting them know where the prey is.

3     Birds are not mammals, and they lay eggs. They are covered in feathers and have beaks for mouths. They do not have hands either, but only stiff wings. Birds can hunt during the day or night, but either way they use their eyes to locate prey.

4     Of course, bats and birds do share many traits. They both fly and have streamlined bodies to help them do so. In addition, both animals are insect eaters and spend time caring for their young.

5     The Venn diagram on the next page compares birds and bats. The information in the circle on the left describes bats, and the information in the circle on the right describes birds. The information in the center describes both bats *and* birds.

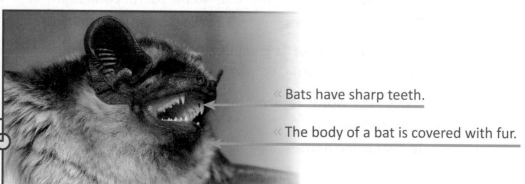

« Bats have sharp teeth.

« The body of a bat is covered with fur.

» Birds are insect eaters.

## Bats

- hunt using sound
- are mammals
- have hands
- have teeth
- have fur
- bear live young

⌃ Bats use echolocation to hunt prey.

- can fly
- have wings
- have streamlined bodies
- care for their young
- eat insects

## Birds

- are not mammals
- have no hands
- have beaks
- have feathers
- lay eggs
- hunt using sight

# Q UESTIONS

_____ 1. **Which of these is TRUE of birds, based on the Venn diagram?**
   (A) They have hands.          (B) They care for their young.
   (C) They hunt using sound.    (D) They are mammals.

_____ 2. **Which of these is TRUE of bats, based on the Venn diagram?**
   (A) They have beaks.          (B) They hunt using sight.
   (C) They eat birds.           (D) They have teeth.

_____ 3. **Which of these is TRUE of both bats and birds?**
   (A) They are not mammals.     (B) They hunt using sound.
   (C) They have wings.          (D) They don't care for their young.

_____ 4. **Which of these is NOT true of birds?**
   (A) They have beaks.          (B) They are not mammals.
   (C) They have fur.            (D) They don't have hands.

_____ 5. **Which of these is NOT true of bats?**
   (A) They are covered in feathers.  (B) They eat insects.
   (C) They hunt at night.            (D) They have teeth.

# 50 Chocolate Heaven in 8 Simple Steps!

**1**     Chocolate mousse is one of my favorite desserts. It is smooth, rich, and so delicious. What's more, I can have it any time I like because it is also very simple to make! All that you need is good quality chocolate, eggs, milk, butter, and sugar. And after just a few simple steps, I can enjoy a heavenly bowl of chocolate mousse!

**2**     Here is the recipe I use to make this delicious dessert. A recipe is a list of steps that shows you how to make a dish. It tells you the ingredients you will need and what to do with them one step at a time.

## Chocolate Mousse

**Serves: 2**

**Time:**   **10 minutes to make (plus 2 hours in the fridge)**

**You will need:**

- **175 grams of good quality chocolate**
- **1 ½ tablespoons of milk**
- **1 ½ tablespoons of butter**
- **3 eggs**
- **1 ½ tablespoons of sugar**

## Q UESTIONS

_____ 1. **How much chocolate do you need to make this recipe?**
(A) Three grams.
(B) Ten grams.
(C) One hundred and seventy-five grams.
(D) One hundred grams.

_____ 2. **How much chocolate mousse does this recipe make?**
(A) Enough for two people.     (B) Enough for three people.
(C) Enough for ten people.     (D) Enough for eight people.

UNIT

4

Final Review

4-4

Review: Reference Sources

Step ❶ Cut up the chocolate into small pieces.

Step ❷ Heat up the milk in a small pan. Add the chocolate and stir until it melts. Then turn off the heat.

Step ❸ Melt the butter (you can do this in the microwave) and add it to the chocolate.

Step ❹ Break the eggs. Separate the yolks from the whites and keep them in different bowls.

Step ❺ Add the sugar to the egg yolks and mix. Then add this mixture to the chocolate. Stir well.

Step ❻ Beat the egg whites until they become stiff. Then fold them gently into the chocolate mixture.

Step ❼ Spoon your mousse into bowls and then cool in the fridge for two hours.

Step ❽ Serve and enjoy!

≫ heating up milk in a pan

≫ separating the yolks from the whites

_____ 3. **What is the first thing you should do when making this recipe?**
 (A) Break the eggs.  (B) Melt the butter.
 (C) Heat up the milk.  (D) Cut up the chocolate.

_____ 4. **After you break the eggs, what should you do with the yolks and the whites?**
 (A) Mix them together.  (B) Put them in the fridge.
 (C) Put them in different bowls.  (D) Heat them up.

_____ 5. **If you start making this recipe at midday (12 p.m.), when will you be able to eat your chocolate mousse?**
 (A) At 2:00 p.m.  (B) At 2:10 p.m.  (C) At 1:30 p.m.  (D) At 1:00 p.m.

# Translation

## Unit 1 | 閱讀技巧

### 1-1 歸納要旨／找出支持性細節

**01 看見它、達成它！** P. 20

你是否有想達到的特別目標？也許你想一星期讀一本書，也許你想在班上名列前茅，或者是加入學校的體育校隊。問題是，你的目標可能沒那麼容易達成，一不小心就有可能會半途而廢，此時你需要願景板來助你一臂之力。

願景板是指將可呼應目標的圖片收集展示。每天看到這些圖片，就能讓你保持專注在自己的目標上。以下是如何以四個簡單步驟製作出自己的願景板。

**1. 選擇目標**

選幾個對你來說很重要的目標，可以是多喝水這類的小目標，或是學習一種新語言等規模較大的目標。要是你的目標規模較大，將其細分成若干階段會有助於目標的選擇。

**2. 搜尋圖片**

搜尋能呼應目標的圖片。你可以上網搜尋圖片，然後列印出來，或者把舊書和雜誌上的圖片剪下來用。

**3. 設計版面**

用膠帶或膠水將圖片黏貼在願景板上，你也可以在空白處寫上一些鼓勵的話，例如「繼續加油！」。

**4. 使用願景板！**

將你的願景板放在每天都會看到的地方，像是房間的牆面上。每天早上，花一分鐘的時間專注地看著願景板，想一想你的目標，想一想你為達成目標而正在做的事。

**02 出售草莓點心棒** P. 22

「我的零嘴」全天然點心棒〔盒裝〕‧‧‧‧‧‧‧‧‧‧‧‧‧‧‧

☆☆☆☆☆　　　總評論數：**35** 則

總重量：**228** 克　每盒點心棒數量：**12** 支

| 草莓　台幣 **1,200** 元 | 香蕉　台幣 **1,200** 元 |

**3** 月 **31** 日前訂購可享免運優惠！

關於此品項

「我的零嘴」點心棒既健康又美味，適合於早餐或作為日常點心享用。

本公司生產的點心棒皆採用天然食材，我們也希望成分單純，所以點心棒僅以三種食材製成：果乾、蜂蜜和燕麥，絕不添加任何非天然的香料。我們認為，最美味的食物永遠來自於高品質且天然的食材，而我們百分之百肯定，您會贊同我們的理念。

本公司在食材來源的選擇上也十分謹慎，我們只與不會破壞環境的農家合作。您在食用「我的零嘴」點心棒時，可以放心您不是跟傷害地球的商家購買產品。

我們的點心棒能在您每次覺得精神不濟時，讓您活力大增。還有，點心棒的大小適中，剛好可以放在您的包包裡隨身攜帶。要是您感到疲憊了，就隨時拿一支出來吃吧！那麼您就會有足夠的精力來撐過今天剩下的時間！

每盒內含 12 支點心棒，每支只要新台幣 100 元！那麼您還在等什麼呢？嚐嚐「我的零嘴」吧！

## 03 下半場更精彩？ P. 24

旁白 1：下半場現在要開打了。目前的比數是東城隊兩分，南城隊零分。南城隊如果想要贏得今天這場重要的球賽，可得好好努力一番了。

旁白 2：沒錯。南城隊至目前為止的表現都不佳，他們的後衛一直讓東城隊的前鋒越過防守，而他們自己的前鋒根本也不怎麼積極。希望下半場他們可以開始打得更有氣勢。我敢說他們的教練米契・麥當勞在中場休息的時候就已經對他們說了重話。

旁白 1：我們來看看球員是否有把教練的話聽進去。球賽開打了，現在是南城隊發球。球在布朗那裡，他把球傳給史密斯。史密斯正一路往東城隊的球門跑去，但是東城隊的後衛來了！羅伯茲要鏟球，但史密斯身手敏捷地從旁閃了過去。

旁白 2：閃得漂亮！史密斯展現了精湛的球技，但他也有辦法躲過另一個後衛瓊斯嗎？史密斯和瓊斯，現在面對面了。史密斯覺得危險，就把球傳給馬丁斯。馬丁斯發現了敵人的破綻。現在就只有他和守門員對戰。他射門，他進球得分了！

旁白 1：好精采的射門！下半場剛開場幾分鐘，南城隊就把比數拉到了二比一。球隊表現的差距也太大了吧！簡直像是另一個完全不同的球隊。如果他們繼續維持這樣的表現，最終很有可能贏得這場比賽！

## 04 照顧自己 P. 26

做一個用功的學生當然是一件好事。不過，你有時可能太過於專注念書，而不敢給自己休個假。這樣的讀書方式可能會導致身體生病，所以在日常生活作息中納入能幫助你放鬆的活動，真的很重要。在朝著學習目標努力的同時，你可以進行以下三件事情來維持你的身心健康。

1. 犒賞自己——別人不見得會知道你很用功讀書，所以他們不一定會因此而獎勵你。然而，重點在於你肯定自己的努力。你知道自己一直都很用功念書，那就可以犒賞自己，對自己好一點，例如享受美味的甜點、和朋友一起消磨時間或是打個電玩遊戲。

2. 暫停一下——當你覺得讀書的壓力越來越大，可以試著騰出時間，遠離書本，好好放鬆一下自己。你要是沒辦法真的去度個假，那就儘量讓自己遠離社群媒體。去掉所有的「雜訊」能給自己留出一些迫切需要的喘息空間。

3. 散步——科學家已經證明，散步可降低壓力程度，讓你頭腦清晰，並使得晚上更好睡。簡而言之，每天走點路，對你的心理健康有很大的益處。

希望藉由執行以上三件簡單的事，你就能達到學習目標，同時維持健康的心態。切記，雖然在意自己的學業是好事，但是照顧好自己也很重要！

「你不了解我，爸」我大吼。
「你老了、脾氣暴躁又刻薄。
你根本不懂我的感受——
不懂一個青少年的感受！」

我跺著腳回到自己房間，氣得臉都紅了，
我砰的一聲甩上門。
我討厭他，我討厭他，我討厭他。我這麼想著。
他就是不懂我是什麼樣的人。

我們是兩個不同的物種，來自兩個不同的星球
兩者相隔百萬光年之遙。
我們是蘋果和橘子、貓和狗。
他是科學，我是藝術。

有人敲了我的房門。我母親走進房間，
她手裡拿著一本書。
「我可以給你看一下這個嗎？」她笑著問。
我聳聳肩，同意看一下。

我打開本子——裡面有些照片
照片上是個跟我年紀差不多的少年。
他跟朋友開懷大笑，看起來很酷的樣子
畫面一頁又一頁地閃過。

這張是他在海邊衝浪的照片。
這張是他在彈吉他的照片。
這張是他頭髮染成綠色的照片。
他看起來像個青澀的搖滾明星！

「這個小孩是誰？」我問母親。
她說：「什麼？你不認得這小子？」
我搖搖頭，我真的不知道。
「孩子啊，這個人，就是你爸！」

---

## 1-2 理解因果關係／釐清寫作技巧

### 06 全體同學請注意！　P. 30

**松景國中**
**第 12 屆年度科學展**

　　全體同學請注意！大家想要幫忙拯救地球嗎？今年的科學展主題是「呵護我們的星球」。所有就讀松景國中的學生皆可參加。參展的專題必須提出本校在保護環境上所能做出的改變。學生可選擇單獨參展，或以團體方式參展。請注意，學生僅能就一項專題參展，參與多項專題的學生將失去參展資格。

**參展方法：**

1. 填妥科學展表格。
2. 請自然科老師在參展表格上簽名。
3. 請家長在表格上簽名。若為團體參展者，所有家長均務必在表格上簽名。
4. 請在 4 月 18 日前將參展表格交給自然科老師。

本次科展的活動時間為 5 月 18 日晚上六點至七點。參展學生應於下午五點半至圖書館布置展覽。展覽期間，參展學生務必全程守候在自己的專題旁，並準備好隨時回答評審的提問。晚上七點將宣布獲獎者。

**第一名**

- 可獲邀參加六月舉辦的市立科學展
- 可於本校自助餐廳消費的 50 元禮品卡

**第二名**

- 可獲邀參加六月舉辦的市立科學展
- 可於本校自助餐廳消費的 25 元禮品卡

**第三名**

- 可獲邀參加六月舉辦的市立科學展

如有任何疑問，請與自然科老師洽詢。

## 07 友情變質時　P. 32

不是每一段友誼都能維持一輩子。

有時候，朋友就是會逐漸疏遠了，而這通常發生在大家年紀漸長，彼此的興趣改變了，或是有人搬家時。

但有的時候，朋友之間會不歡而散、惡言相向。14 歲的艾拉就遇到這樣的情況，她發現她的「閨蜜」琪琪並不是什麼好人。

艾拉說：「我們那時跟幾個女生在公園裡，琪琪試圖排擠我，不讓我參與她們。然後她針對我的穿著說了一些尖酸刻薄的話，大家哄堂大笑。隔天，我跟琪琪說她讓我很難過，但她沒說對不起。事實上，她還說我是『魯蛇』。」

這兩個女孩從二年級開始就是朋友，所以艾拉對於失去琪琪這件事感到很痛苦。但她清楚知道，她們這段友情無法再延續下去了。

「朋友之間本該互相關心。雖然我意識到琪琪不再是我真正的朋友了，但我還是會想念她，我花了好幾個月的時間才交新朋友，那段時間蠻孤單的。」

如果你也遇到相同情況，請記得，這不是世界末日！當一段友情變質時，請參考以下建議：

- 接受無常，並非事事永恆長存。
- 明白沒有那個尖酸刻薄的人相伴，你的人生會更美好。
- 對你們曾經擁有的開心回憶感恩。
- 思考一下，你可以從這件事學到什麼課題。
- 不斷告訴自己有多棒！
- 一旦你覺得自己準備好了，就開始花時間與他人相處。

## 08 非常炎熱的話題　P. 34

**男孩：** 老天，我今天簡直是汗如雨下！最近的天氣實在熱到不行。

**女孩：** 我覺得今天稍早的氣溫差不多逼近 40 度，我很高興家裡有冷氣可以吹。

**男孩：** 我也是。要是沒有冷氣的話，我真的不知道要怎麼活下去。嘿，你知道在歐洲幾乎沒有人會在家裡安裝冷氣嗎？

**女孩：** 他們不裝冷氣嗎？但我看新聞說，那邊的氣溫跟今年這裡的夏季氣溫一樣高了。

**男孩：** 我其實有問我住在英國的表親這個問題。他說，這是因為之前他們不太需要冷氣。雖然以前的夏天確實會很熱，但從來不會熱到難以忍受。歐洲那邊的房子通常是為了在漫長嚴寒的冬天保持溫暖而設計的，而不是為了能夠在夏天感到涼爽的設計的。

**女孩：** 有道理。但現在隨著氣溫逐年攀升，我想他們會開始需要冷氣了。

**男孩：** 是啊，我表親說，現在有越來越多人買冷氣，他家最近才剛裝好，他說家裡一天 24 小時冷氣都開著。

**女孩：** 你應該跟他說，要等熱到不行的時候再開冷氣，否則他會對冷氣上癮，最後用電量會很大。這就是為什麼我爸每天只讓我們在氣溫最熱的時候，才吹幾個小時冷氣的原因。

## `09` 無線網路背後的女性推手　P. 36

　　她被譽為「電影界最美的女性」，不過，海蒂・拉瑪有的可不僅僅是一張漂亮的臉蛋而已。生於 1914 年的拉瑪，是美國知名的電影女演員，但她也很喜歡發明東西。儘管她沒有接受過正規的科學訓練，她的點子卻改變了我們連接網路的方式，可以說如果沒有她，無線網路可能就不存在了！

　　拉瑪從小到大都是家中的獨生女，所以她的父親對她疼愛有加。拉瑪的父親對科技十分好奇，父女倆會一起討論機器運作方式，一聊就是好幾個數小時。因此，拉瑪對這類主題也產生了濃厚的興趣，她甚至開始拆解自己的玩具，就為了想知道玩具是怎麼組裝起來的。

　　即使她後來是以演員的身分成名，但她仍然保持著對發明的興趣。在第二次世界大戰期間，她和某個朋友開發了一種隱藏無線電波的新方法，其目的是阻止敵人用無線電控制的魚雷進行干擾。不過，美國海軍最後並未採用他們的構想。

　　令人惋惜的是，過了很多年以後，大家這才開始明白她的發明有多重要。不過，她的構想繼續啟發許多現代科技，包括無線網路。2014 年，也就是她離世的 14 年後，拉瑪終於因其偉大的發明而登上「美國發明家名人堂」。

## `10` 沖馬桶前先蓋馬桶蓋！　P. 38

# 先蓋馬桶蓋，再沖水！
**馬桶沖水前一定要先蓋上馬桶蓋的原因。**

雷恩・奧斯曼 撰

　　你上廁所的時候，可能會按部就班地進行這幾個步驟。首先，你會先上廁所，然後沖馬桶，最後是洗手和擦乾雙手。大功告成！你的雙手都很乾淨的，你的「大小便」現已在遙遠的地下管道裡。可真的是這樣嗎？其實，有一層薄薄的「大小便物質」正附著在你身上——在你全身上下的衣物上，甚至在你的頭髮上，還附著在你的毛巾上、你的牙刷上，以及在一切你拿進廁所的物品上，例如你的手機。

　　但是，它究竟是怎麼附著到物品上的呢？這個嘛，在你按下沖水鈕沖馬桶的時候，產生的沖力會將馬桶裡物質（如糞便）的微粒排放到空氣中。研究顯示，這些微粒可傳播到幾乎離馬桶兩公尺遠的地方！我知道這很噁心。而且要是你和病人共用一間廁所，然後又觸碰到沾了他們糞便微粒的東西會怎麼樣？事實證明，沖馬桶是同住者之間傳播疾病的絕佳方法。

那麼你該怎麼辦？幸好有解決方法。只要在沖馬桶前，把馬桶蓋蓋上就行了！如此便能將所有物質安穩地留在馬桶裡。三不五時消毒一下馬桶蓋仍是個好辦法，不過蓋上馬桶蓋能使廁所裡的其他地方，以及你的衣物、頭髮、牙刷和手機等，都會是令人開心的「便便零沾染」狀態。

## 1-3 作者的目的及語氣／做出推測

### 11 嶄新的書香世界 P. 40

**3 月 14 日 星期一**

　　上個月我寫了加入讀書會這件事，今天是第一次的聚會，我讀了一本名為《漫漫征途》的書。內容講的是某個少年橫跨美國的旅程，而故事則是發生在 1930 年代。這本書和我平常會看的書完全不同。我平常都是看惡靈、吸血鬼之類的恐怖小說，但是閱讀到風格如此迥異的小說，我其實也很開心。我很愛看驚悚小說，也看過無數本這類的書了！但我現在很高興能閱讀到新類型的小說。

　　我也知道，我可以從更廣泛的閱讀中，發掘我前所未聞的事物。以閱讀《漫漫征途》為例，我學到了很多美國地理方面的知識，也得知近百年前人們的生活概況。

　　我也很喜歡參加讀書會的人，大家都很友善。還有另外六個人，他們都非常熱情歡迎我、鼓勵我跟他們分享我的想法。我覺得參加讀書會，我變得更有自信，勇於分享自己的意見與想法。這對我在學校的課堂討論很有幫助，因為目前我通常都是讓別人發言。

　　下個月的書目是《偷走月亮的女人》，我已經從圖書館借了一本，等不及要開始閱讀啦！

### 12 夏季游泳須知 P. 42

**在湖泊、河川裡游泳很危險！**

　　夏天到了！很多人都想去戶外游泳，但是在湖泊、河川裡游泳卻是十分危險的。去年，本地就有 120 人在湖泊、河川裡游泳時，發生意外事故或身體健康出了問題。以下是幾個可能會發生的危險情況，你得心裡有數：

| ⚠️ 水裡的尖銳物體 | ⚠️ 冷休克 | ⚠️ 藍綠藻 |
|---|---|---|
| 尖銳的物體，像是湖底或河底的碎瓶子等，有時難以察覺，要是不小心踩到了，可是真的會受傷的。 | 冷水會迅速帶走身體的能量，讓你的手腳僵硬無力，難以游回岸邊。如果周遭無人幫忙，你可能會溺水。 | 水面上出現狀似大片藍綠色斑塊的是細菌。在細菌裡游泳可能會對你的皮膚和眼睛造成傷害。 |

| ⚠️ 水裡的糞便 | ⚠️ 鉤端螺旋體病 |
|---|---|
| 湖泊、河川裡含有大量來自人類和動物的排泄物。如果吞下湖水或河水，就可能會生重病。 | 這是一種因老鼠在水中撒尿而傳播的疾病，還是一種可能致死的嚴重疾病。 |

　　為避免發生上述危險情況，請勿在本地的湖泊與河川裡游泳。大家何不改到本區兩座游泳池中任一座泳池裡游泳呢？那裡保證能提供你一個安全、水質乾淨的游泳體驗！

## 13 送給黃老師的禮物  P. 44

*三名學生正在網路上聊天。*

麥特：大家有沒有想過，我們畢業前要買什麼禮物送給黃老師？

琳達：我想我們可以送他一本歷史方面的書，我們都知道他很愛歷史。

琪琪：這個嘛，他是教歷史的，你不覺得送他歷史書籍有點無趣嗎？我敢肯定，他已經有超
　　　多歷史方面的書了。

琳達：也是，我想你是對的。

麥特：那送一個漂亮的保溫杯怎麼樣？黃老師喜歡喝茶，不是嗎？如果我們送他一個保溫效
　　　果良好的保溫杯，他就可以帶茶到學校，保溫杯可以讓茶保溫一整天。

琪琪：這是個很棒的點子！他絕對會愛上這個禮物。我現在就上網找，大約新台幣 1000 元
　　　就可以買到一個不錯的保溫杯。

麥特：但我們之前講好要花的金額是新台幣 1500 元。除了保溫杯之外，我們還可以送他別
　　　的東西嗎？

琳達：喔！我想到了。我家附近有間賣茶的茶行，我可以挑個新台幣 500 元左右的優質茶葉。
　　　我想一個保溫杯加上一包好茶葉會是一組不錯的禮物。

麥特：太好了。那麼，琪琪，你去訂保溫杯；琳達，你去買茶；我來寫卡片，然後我們都在
　　　卡片上簽名，並在最後一個上學日，把所有的東西都送給黃老師。

琳達：👍

琪琪：👍

## 14 在橡樹飯店住宿一晚  P. 46

收件人：manager@oaktreehotel.com

寄件人：dana.cook@fastmail.com

主旨：糟糕的住宿經歷

親愛的先生／女士：

　　我最近在橡樹飯店住了一個晚上後返家，我當時的住宿體驗並不佳，事實上，我從
來沒有住過這麼糟糕的飯店。

　　房間很髒，地板上還有死蒼蠅，在床上睡一晚後，隔天我的皮膚就很癢。我覺得床單
已經很久沒洗了，我隔壁的房間還傳來震耳欲聾的音樂聲。我打電話到櫃台抱怨的時候，
他們跟我說他們對此無能為力。晚餐我點了客房服務，餐點居然花了一個多小時才送來，
而且還冷冰冰的！

　　我想讓你們知道，我以後絕對不會去住這家飯店了。

唐娜・庫克

收件人：dana.cook@fastmail.com

寄件人：manager@oaktreehotel.com

關於：糟糕的住宿經歷

親愛的庫克小姐：

關於您在本飯店的糟糕經歷，本人深感抱歉。最近我們許多員工都生病了，因此目前僱用很多臨時工。遺憾的是，他們不像我們的正式員工那般訓練有素。

我們會立即退還您的住宿費，希望您可以原諒這些過失。

此外，要跟您說一聲，我們大部分的正式員工很快就會回到工作崗位。我們真的希望您能再次入住本飯店，我們好為您提供更好的住宿經驗。

敬祝安康

經理 理查・瓊斯

## 15 換了文字，就換了顏色 P. 48

想一下彩虹的樣子。你看到了多少種顏色？說英語的人會看到七種顏色：紅、橙、黃、綠、藍、靛、紫。不過，巴布亞紐幾內亞一國裡說大尼語的人，則只會看到「mili」和「mola」這兩種顏色。「mili」是指彩虹裡「偏暖色調」的部分（即英語人士所說的紅色、橙色、黃色）；「mola」則是「偏冷色調」的部分（即綠色、藍色等）。這真是一個既奇特又有趣的事實：我們看著一模一樣的顏色，但看到的顏色卻會因所使用的語言而異。

再舉個例子說明。請想像一下萬里無雲的天空以及一顆藍莓的樣子，英語人士會說「兩者都是藍色」。雖然其中一個是淺藍色，而另一個是深藍色，但仍統稱藍色。不過，說希臘語的人，卻不認同這樣的說法。對希臘人而言，天空是「ghalazio」（較淺的藍色），藍莓則是「ble」（較深的藍色），這可是兩種截然不同的顏色！不過，現在有個令人意外的現象，住在英語系國家的希臘人，久而久之會逐漸認為「ghalazio」和「ble」這兩種顏色愈來愈相似，將這兩種顏色歸類為「藍色」的英語講法，一步步改變了他們的思維模式！

不僅顏色方面會有此現象，科學家亦已證明，我們看待事情的方式和語言文字有關，如空間、數字與性別等。這讓人不禁想問：到底是我們自己，還是文字在控制我們的思維？到頭來，我們的思想也許並沒有我們想像中的那麼自由。

## 1-4 綜合技巧練習

## 16 意想不到的夥伴 P. 50

槲寄生是一種靠竊取大樹養料與水分而生存的植物。它的種子會降落在樹枝上，然後開始汲取生長所需的養分。但是槲寄生的種子最初是怎麼跑到那麼高的地方的呢？種子當然不會飛！答案是：槲寄生利用會飛的小夥伴將它的種子帶到高聳的樹梢枝頭上。而這個夥伴就是眾所周知的槲寄生鳥（譯註：又名澳洲啄花鳥）！

槲寄生鳥分布於澳洲和印尼的部分地區，牠們喜歡吃槲寄生的漿果。這些漿果有一層厚厚的外皮保護，但是槲寄生鳥以其堅硬的喙嘴，輕易地在果皮上撕開一個洞，然後使勁地捏住果實，裡面美味的漿果就會直接爆漿。對這種體型不大的小鳥來說，大顆漿果可說是很有飽足感的一餐。

　　漿果隨後就會通過槲寄生鳥的消化系統。不過，漿果中間的種子並不會被消化分解掉，大約三十分鐘後，黏黏的種子就會從槲寄生鳥的另一端整個完好地被排泄出來。槲寄生鳥接下來會用樹枝擦屁股，把黏呼呼的種子擦掉，種子隨即在樹枝上生根發芽並開始生長。

　　如此循環往復，作為植物的槲寄生為槲寄生鳥提供了食物，而槲寄生鳥則確保槲寄生的種子找到一個生長的好去處，多麼便利的合作關係呀！

## 17 親愛的爸爸　P. 52

親愛的爸爸：

　　父親節快樂！我想寫張紙條跟你說，我是多麼感激你為我所做的一切。因為有你，我才有舒服的地方住，而且從來沒有挨過餓，我可以沒有任何後顧之憂的專注在課業上。

　　我知道你很辛苦，一個人不但照顧我，還要做全職的工作。有時候我看得出來你下班回家後有多麼累，但卻從未抱怨，還教我功課。即使你的工作很忙，你總會想方設法為我騰出時間來。我知道這樣很辛苦，但我想讓你知道我有多麼喜歡跟你待在一起。

　　但從現在開始，我希望你也可以多照顧自己一點。我會竭盡所能的幫忙做家事，也許有時幫我倆煮頓晚餐，這樣你下班回家後就可以稍微放鬆一下了。我也可以去和爺爺奶奶家住幾個週末，那樣你就能好好休息，做些自己喜歡的事。你對我來說很重要，我希望你身體健康、幸福快樂。

非常愛你的兒子
卡爾 敬上

## 18 色彩的影響力　P. 54

　　我們的情緒和行為會被周遭色彩影響嗎？很多人覺得會。有人喜歡把房間粉刷成藍色，因為他們覺得藍色能使人平靜；速食餐廳則常被粉刷成紅色和黃色，這是因為據說紅色能讓人感到肚子餓，而黃色則能讓人感到快樂與親切；有些國家的監獄牢房會粉刷成粉紅色，因為聽說粉紅色會讓人比較不會逞兇鬥狠。

　　我們很容易就能聯想到，上述顏色會讓我們做出某些行為的原因。例如，藍色大概會讓人想到美麗夏日裡晴朗無雲的天空，或是寧靜無波的海洋。紅色是許多水果成熟後的顏色，如蘋果、草莓、番茄等。當你產生這樣的聯想時，就會覺得很有道理。

　　科學家已經多次試圖在測試中證明這些說法。然而，測試結果不是很可靠。每當某項測試結果「證明」了某種顏色會對人產生某種影響時，隨後進行的類似測試就會推翻此一說法。那麼，會發生這種情況的真相到底是什麼？

　　有可能只是因為色彩對我們每個人的影響是高度因人而異的，並沒有規則可循。目前科學家們正在策劃更好的測試辦法，好釐清問題的真相。不過，可能還需要一段時間，我們才會知道色彩影響我們的原因和途徑，或究竟色彩是否真的對我們有一丁點影響。

## 19 有了這項能力，凡事近乎可能　P. 56

自律是一個人所能擁有最棒的能力。自律是什麼意思？意思就是能夠克制自己並控制自己的行為，還意味著能夠做對的事、避免養成壞習慣的能力（例如，浪費時間）。以學生來說，這表示你會在打電動之前寫完作業；表示雖然你知道偷偷跟朋友聊天更好玩，但上課的時候還是會專心聽講；表示你會放下手機去讀那本重要的書。

但是實話實說吧，自律不容易做到啊，壞習慣往往令人難以抗拒。的確，要做到自律，就必須擁有強大的意志力。雖然沒有人天生就擁有強大的自律能力，但自律是可以培養的，培養自律的方式就跟上手某項運動或樂器的方法一樣——透過練習。

從小處著手是個不錯的辦法，例如，每天在同一時間起床，然後逐漸給自己設定更艱難的挑戰。還要留意自己的優缺點，弄清楚什麼會讓你分心（也許是因為手機就在身邊）、什麼會讓你感到有動力（也許是聽音樂），然後善用這些來幫助自己建立自律的能力。

當你越來越有自律力，你會開始覺得更能自我克制了。你會越來越成功，而以往那些看似不可能的目標似乎突然變得唾手可得。正如美國偉大的總統羅斯福曾說的，「有了自律，凡事近乎可能！」

## 20 自帶杯子，拯救地球　P. 58

今晚的下一則新聞與環境有關，也與多家飲料店為減少垃圾而採取的積極措施有關。

我們都知道，購買飲料時所使用的塑膠杯或紙杯所產生的垃圾量有多少。因此，為了實現零垃圾的目標，國內各地許多咖啡店和手搖店主動為自備飲料杯的顧客提供優惠折扣。

**查爾斯・史密斯　國王咖啡店老闆**

我們不希望成為地球受汙染的幫兇，因此在今年年初，我們開始為自帶杯子買飲料的顧客打九折。從那時起，本店使用的杯子數量就減少了 25%，這是很棒的成效。當然，我們希望此數字可以降更多。

**奧莉維亞・阿里　常客**

我早上去上班的途中會買咖啡，然後下班回家的路上會買奶茶。我以前不曾自備飲料杯，但是在很多商家開始提供自備飲料杯的折扣後，我就去買了一個可以重複使用的飲料杯，現在我去買飲料都會帶著去。我每天不僅省到錢，還為拯救地球盡一份力，這樣的感覺很棒！

政府在得知上述店家的做法後，如今也在努力讓更多店家效法。我們會在接下來的幾個月，繼續關注此事。

# Unit 2 | 字彙學習

## 認識同義字與反義字／從上下文推測字義

**21 捐血救人** P. 62

### 為什麼要捐血？

想要救人一命，血液極其重要。血液能讓人從重大的事故、手術，甚至是罹癌的情況下存活下來。醫院需要大量的血液，還需要所有的血型。不過現在，能夠捐血的人之中，只有 3% 的人會去捐血。

### 通常只要滿足以下條件，就能捐血

- 健康概況良好，且身體沒有不舒服。
- 16 歲以上、65 歲以下。
- 體重至少 50 公斤。

### 捐血前的準備

- 前一晚睡飽。
- 捐血前至少 24 小時未服用任何藥物。
- 吃飽吃好，但避免油膩食物。
- 大量喝水。

### 捐血的程序

1. 出示身分證並填妥捐血表。
2. 檢測血型。
3. 測量體重。
4. 回答醫生的問題。
5. 捐血（約需 10 分鐘）。

### 捐血後的注意事項

- 休息 5 至 10 分鐘。
- 馬上喝點水、吃些點心。
- 接下來的一天，請勿進行劇烈運動。
- 泡澡或淋浴的水溫請勿過熱。
- 如果覺得頭暈，請立刻躺下。
- 下一餐請吃些富含鐵質的食物。

請上網搜尋距離您最近的捐血據點：www.giveblood.com

**22 簡單卻重要的觸碰** P. 64

或許你在寶萊塢電影或印度的電視劇中看過這個動作：年輕人會彎下腰去觸碰長者的腳。對於不熟悉印度傳統的人來說，此舉可能看起來很奇怪。這樣的姿態是什麼意思？為什麼觸碰的是腳，而不是手呢？

觸碰長者的腳是一項古老的傳統。事實上，大概從三千年前就開始了！對印度超過十億人的印度教徒而言，這種行為象徵高度敬意。彎腰，有時是跪下或趴著的動作，能讓自己的位置低於長者。而這樣的位置，表示你肯定這樣的人比你更有經驗與智慧。

而長者被摸腳後的回禮，就是祝福你。觸碰長者的腳，對於尋求智慧、良好健康狀態或好運的人而言，是十分重要的舉動。因此，印度教徒常會在重要場合觸碰長者的腳，例如慶生會與婚禮。他們也會在面臨艱鉅任務前，以此方式尋求祝福，例如要長途旅行或考試。

孩童自小就被教導此項傳統，因此，多數印度人是在十分尊重長者的環境下長大。也許這是一個簡單的動作，但是確實教會了印度年輕人非常重要的課題。

## 23 羅馬數字計數法 P. 66

　　觀察一下某些時鐘的鐘面，你會發現上面的時標刻度並不是以 1、2、3、4 等數字來表示幾點鐘，而是以 I、II、III、IV 等符號來呈現。你也許會納悶：「為什麼要寫成這麼奇怪的樣子呢？」這是因為時鐘上的數字經常是以羅馬數字書寫的。

　　羅馬數字是大約兩千年前的古羅馬時期數字書寫的方式，對於現代人來說，這個系統可能有點難以理解，但是稍微練習一下，就會變得越來越容易理解。首先要記住，數值 1 是以字母「I」表示，5 是以字母「V」表示，10 是以字母「X」表示。接下來，2 會被寫成「1 加上 1」，也就是「II」；4 會被寫成「比 5 少 1」，也就是「IV」。同理，6 是「5 加上 1」，也就是「VI」；9 是「比 10 少 1」，也就是「IX」。最後，11 是「10 加上 1」，也就是「XI」，以此類推。有人說，這些數字是牧羊人發明的，他們用來數綿羊的。每數一隻羊，就在木頭上刻一刀（I）；每數到第五隻羊，就刻兩刀（V）；每數到第十隻就刻一個叉（X）。

　　我們現今鮮少使用羅馬數字來計數。其實，這個系統存在一些瑕疵，其一就是沒有代表「零」的符號。然而，偶爾還是會有人用羅馬數字。例如，你可能會在書籍裡看到用羅馬數字標示章節數，或是在古老的建築或雕像上看到以羅馬數字標示日期。現在，你再看到這些奇怪的符號時，就不會再覺得它們很神秘了！

## 24 岩石形成的波浪 P. 68

西澳＞伯斯＞一日遊

# 波浪岩

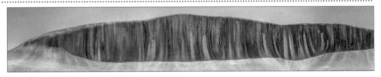

　　您可能會納悶，波浪在離海洋 300 多公里遠的地方做什麼？此波浪並非由水形成的，而是由岩石形成的！波浪岩是西澳最令人讚嘆的自然景觀之一，看起來宛如被時間凍結的巨浪。這陣「波浪」有 15 公尺高、100 多公尺長，且黃、棕、灰等色相間。這些深淺不一的色澤，看起來彷彿是陽光照耀在滾滾而來的浪濤上。當然，這陣波浪哪也去不了——事實上，波浪岩已在此處 6000 多萬年了。

**最佳觀賞時間**：春季，當地許多美麗花卉皆於此時開始綻放。

**交通資訊**：波浪岩距離最近的都市伯斯有四小時的車程（340 公里）。每天都有許多觀光巴士從伯斯出發，您可以擇一參加，也可以自行開車前往。

**延長行程**：波浪岩附近可做的事情很多，往北一公里處就是風景優美的夢幻湖，您可在此觀看壯觀的日出。還有一個很好玩的野生動物園區，您可在此看到袋鼠、鹿、珍奇鳥類與其他許多有趣的動物。而打算在此過夜的人，可到波浪岩飯店住宿。

## 25 鯊魚之王 P. 70

　　大白鯊至今仍是世上最大型的鯊魚，牠的長度可生長到六公尺以上。光是想到大白鯊滿嘴如刀片般銳利的牙齒，就會讓很多人怕到不敢下海游泳。但是 1,500 萬年前，大白鯊遠遠稱不上是海洋裡最大隻的鯊魚，當時這個頭銜屬於「巨齒鯊」——也就是史上體型最龐大的鯊魚！

巨齒鯊比一輛公車還大，下顎寬到只需要咬五大口，就可以把一隻鯨魚吃下肚！我們很幸運，因為巨齒鯊大約在 350 萬年前就絕種了。你能想像海裡有這種怪獸游來游去的情況下，我們還在其中游泳、衝浪或航船會有多麼危險嗎？

那麼，這個鯊魚之王為什麼會從海洋中消失呢？雖然有可能是基於若干原因，不過氣候變遷是主要因素。巨齒鯊性喜在溫暖的水域裡生活、捕食獵物，然而，約莫 500 萬年前，地球氣溫開始下降。海洋變得更加寒冷，巨齒鯊可以生存的區域也隨之縮小了，此外，這樣寒冷的氣候也導致許多其他動物死亡——這些動物都是巨齒鯊賴以為生的食物。在這樣的條件下，巨齒鯊根本無法生存。

如今，這些海洋巨獸遺留下來的就只剩下 18 公分長的牙齒化石，這些牙齒有時會被海浪沖到海岸邊。

## 26 將情感化為語言　P. 72

「男生不准哭！」是小男生難過的時候常聽到的話。女生可以自由表達自己的情緒，可男生往往從小就被教導要把情感深藏在心裡。

然而，壓抑自己的情感會導致日後的心理健康問題，也會讓年輕男生的舉止更加暴力，因為他們沒有其他方法來表達自己的感受。男生如果試著表達自己的情感，有時會被說成是弱者，但真的不是這樣，表達自己真正的感受需要很大的勇氣。再者，這麼做能讓自己感覺更被了解、更能掌控自己的情緒。簡而言之，這是一件非常正面的事。

那麼該怎麼做呢？第一步就是花點時間思考一下，你到底感受到什麼樣的情緒。儘量具體化，然後試著思考，自己為什麼會有這樣的感受。當你的腦子裡有完整的想法時，請大聲說出口。如果你不習慣表達自己的感受，可能會很難達成，但是透過練習就能做到。此外，一定要表達自己正面的感受，負面感受亦然。表達正面感受能幫你與所愛之人建立更堅固的情感連結，還會讓你自我感覺更好。

想想看，如果只是因為你是個男孩，就錯失上述這些超棒的好處，似乎有點傻。所以，不管你是什麼性別，都要勇於表達自己！你絕對不會後悔！

## 27 準備迎接三木書展　P. 74

2023 年 3 月 2 日～4 日 上午 10 點～下午 4 點

### 三木圖書即將來到希爾敦學校

我們很興奮地宣布 2023 年三木書展的消息！敬邀希爾敦學校的學生參觀本公司在學校足球場設攤的展位，我們精心挑選了世界知名作家所撰寫的上百本精采著作。

大家喜歡閱讀什麼樣的題材？和遙遠星球上的外星人來一趟刺激的太空冒險嗎？在令人毛骨悚然的房子裡發生的鬼故事嗎？兩人墜入愛河的愛情故事嗎？有趣的異國旅遊日記嗎？我們的書展應有盡有！

如需於到訪博覽會之前參閱所有書單，請至網站 www.threetreespublishing.com/book-list。大家可在網站找到所有書目的資訊。

如欲訂購書籍，請向你的老師索取「圖書訂購單」。請填寫書籍資訊，並交給老師，如此便能確保你在書展能買到心儀的書籍。

更多好消息！
由於我們想鼓勵年輕人閱讀，因此所有商品一律八折出售！所以，快來書展瞧瞧吧，你也許會發現新歡唷！

## 28 睡得好，才能保持警覺 P. 76

事實顯示，一個人所能做的最有礙身體健康的事情，就是睡眠過少。研究指出，睡眠時間過短會導致各種嚴重的健康問題，例如心臟病與癌症。然而，沒幾個人知道，每天睡眠不足對大腦的影響有多嚴重。

看看以下的研究結果吧，絕對會嚇你一跳。僅僅 17 個小時沒有睡覺後，你的警覺度幾乎等於法律認定的喝醉狀態！24 小時沒有睡覺後，你的警覺度就跟喝了好幾杯酒的人一樣，但是你甚至不需要做出上述極端行為，就能達到這樣的效果。只要晚上經常性地少睡幾個小時，也會有此現象。比方說，連續十天每晚只睡六小時，對大腦造成的影響跟 24 個小時沒有睡覺是一樣的。而且，這個影響還無法靠睡一晚好覺來抵銷，你必須好好地睡飽三個晚上，才有辦法恢復正常！

簡而言之，如果你真的想要盡其所能地展現自身才華，就得挪出時間來睡覺。每晚睡七到九個小時是最理想的。擁有這樣的休息量，你會驚訝地發現，自己的思緒竟變得更加清晰了！

## 29 現在或飯後？ P. 78

大家都知道服用維他命有益身體健康，但你是否也知道其服用時間和服用方式一樣重要？以下是各種維他命的最佳服用時間點和方式。

→ 維他命 B 和 C 是水溶性的，意指可在水中分解，讓人體吸收，最好在早餐前或是兩餐之間服用。維他命 C 亦能幫助人體吸收鐵質，所以應該一起服用。

→ 有些維他命是脂溶性，所以需要油脂才能溶解，包括維他命 A、D、E 和 K 等。這類維他命應與含有脂肪的食物或零食一起服用，像是堅果、蛋和起司等。

→ 綜合維他命同時有水溶性的維他命和脂溶性的維他命，所以應該和食物一起服用，如此便可讓脂溶性維他命分解，而對水溶性維他命的吸收影響輕微。

→ 鎂不是一種維他命，但是對人體的健康很重要。任何的時間點都可以服用鎂，雖然有些人空腹服用會覺得胃不太舒服。

簡而言之，維他命是要搭配食物一起服用或空腹來服用，比服用的時間點重要。空腹時服用水溶性維他命，用餐時服用脂溶性維他命，就能讓你的身體以最有成效與效率的方式處理這些維他命。

## 30 氣味大師 P. 80

在隨便一家香水公司裡，最重要的人物絕對是調香師（the nose）。雖然「nose」聽起來不像職稱，更像是身體的某個部位，但是俗稱「鼻子」的調香師是負責創造出公司知名香水的人。就像畫家會結合不同的色彩來作畫一樣，調香師也會調和不同的氣味來創作香水。

調香師需要具備豐富的專業知識，以及絕佳的嗅覺。他們必須能夠辨識出上千種不同的氣味，並了解彼此之間的交互作用為何。他們還需要知道氣味隨著時間推移會產生何種變化，又會帶給人什麼樣的感受。當香水公司想要出一款新香水時，他們就會向調香師描述此香水的氣味，以及希望它帶給人們什麼樣的感覺。一個優秀的調香師能夠挑選出所需的成分，予以調和，將對新款香水的奇思妙想付諸實踐。

要成為調香師並非易事。現今，調香師大多需要取得化學方面的高等學位，然後才能開始接受香水業的培訓。不過，天道酬勤，如果調香師最終真的創作出一款優異的香水，那麼在未來幾年裡，將會行銷到世界各地數百萬人的手中，歷久不衰。

# Unit 3 學習策略

## 3-1 影像圖表

### 31 水力發電！ P. 84

聽到「可再生能源」一詞時，你的腦海中浮現出什麼？風力發電？還是太陽能發電？這幾種都是大家耳熟能詳的可再生能源，可能是因為它們最醒目的關係吧。畢竟，巨大的渦輪風力發電機以及屋頂上滿滿的太陽能板，著實令人無法視而不見！但還有另一種可再生能源經常被忽視，那就是以水力產生電能的「水力發電」（譯註：hydropower 即 hydroelectric power）。

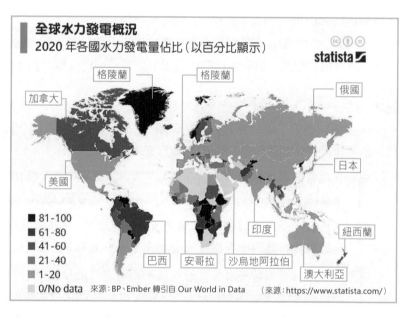

全球水力發電概況
2020 年各國水力發電量佔比（以百分比顯示）

格陵蘭　格陵蘭　俄國
加拿大
美國
日本
■ 81-100
■ 61-80
■ 41-60
■ 21-40
■ 1-20
□ 0/No data
印度　紐西蘭
巴西　安哥拉　沙烏地阿拉伯　澳大利亞
來源：BP、Ember 轉引自 Our World in Data　（來源：https://www.statista.com/）

水力發電是一種既能產生能源又不會傷害地球的好方法。水力發電廠的附近通常水源充沛，發電廠可透過改變水源流量的方式來控制產生多少的電量，如果突然需要大量的電力，只需釋出更多水量即可。目前全世界約有 7% 的電力是來自於水力發電，這比太陽能發電和風力發電加總的百分比還高！事實上，有些國家幾乎完全依賴水力發電。請看下頁地圖，圖中顯示 2020 年世界各國水力發電量的佔比。

### 32 新冠疫情期間的新家園 P. 86

2019 年，美國的動物收容所收留了將近 35 萬隻動物。在同一年裡，卻僅有將近 54% 的動物被領養走。然後，新冠肺炎衝擊了全世界，並且對上述數字產生了莫大的影響。

從 2019 年到 2021 年，進入收容所的動物數量下降到剛剛好超過 26 萬隻，對此驟降情況，我們僅能推測，或許是因在新冠疫情期間，大家不得不待在家裡，而變得更愛自己的寵物。

　　此外，那些在疫情期間最終仍被送到收容所的動物裡，被領養的比例也高出了許多。下頁的折線圖即顯示了此領養數據（折線圖會將表示數字的點狀符號相連起來，以方便判讀某時間範圍內該數字的升降趨勢）。不過想當然爾，有些人未曾經過深思熟慮就從收容所領養動物，隨後不久就又將動物退回給收容所。不過，我們還是希望那些在新冠疫情期間被領養的寵物，真正找到一輩子適合自己的避風港。

## 收容所中被領養的動物百分比（美國）

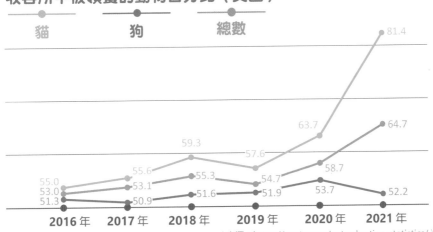

〔來源：https://spots.com/pet-adoption-statistics/〕

**33　全球高齡化最嚴重的國家** P. 88 ..................................................................................

　　兩百年前，普通人的預期壽命僅 40 歲左右，如今，此數字已攀升至 72.98 歲。某些國家的人民甚至有望能活到 80 歲以上！與此同時，許多國家的新生兒數量卻年年下降，這表示某些國家的年長者（即 65 歲（含）以上的人）佔總人口的比例越來越高。這些俗稱「高齡化社會」的國家，面臨著巨大的挑戰，他們必須想方設法地去照顧越來越多的老年人，可是能夠對經濟有所貢獻的年輕人卻偏偏越來越少。

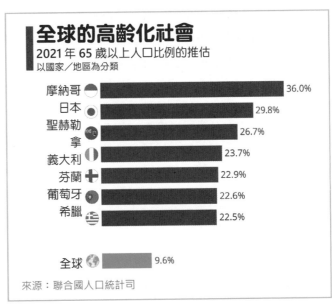

全球的高齡化社會
2021 年 65 歲以上人口比例的推估
以國家／地區為分類

| | |
|---|---|
| 摩納哥 | 36.0% |
| 日本 | 29.8% |
| 聖赫勒拿 | 26.7% |
| 義大利 | 23.7% |
| 芬蘭 | 22.9% |
| 葡萄牙 | 22.6% |
| 希臘 | 22.5% |
| 全球 | 9.6% |

來源：聯合國人口統計司

　　下頁長條圖顯示了世界上某些邁入高齡化社會的國家。長條圖是將數字以不同長度的矩形或長條狀標示出來，數字越大，長條越長。以下頁的圖而言，國家名稱被列在左側，每個國家 65 歲（含）以上的人口比例，則以長條狀的方式顯示在國家名稱旁邊。

**34　空氣最糟的國家** P. 90 ..................................................................................

　　空氣汙染在現代社會是一大問題。汽車、摩托車、貨車與公車會釋放出大量的懸浮微粒到空氣中，而燃燒煤炭、石油與木材同樣也會造成此現象。這些微粒的體積極小，小到即使

**2018 年至 2021 年間，十個空汙最嚴重的國家及其平均空汙濃度（微克／立方公尺）**

| 國家 | 2021 年 | 2020 年 | 2019 年 | 2018 年 |
| --- | --- | --- | --- | --- |
| 孟加拉 | 76.9 | 77.1 | 83.3 | 97.1 |
| 查德 | 75.9 | 無數據 | 無數據 | 無數據 |
| 巴基斯坦 | 66.8 | 59 | 65.8 | 74.3 |
| 塔吉克 | 59.4 | 30.9 | 無數據 | 無數據 |
| 印度 | 58.1 | 51.9 | 58.1 | 72.5 |
| 阿曼 | 53.9 | 44.4 | 無數據 | 無數據 |
| 吉爾吉斯 | 50.8 | 43.5 | 33.2 | 無數據 |
| 巴林 | 49.8 | 39.7 | 46.8 | 59.8 |
| 伊拉克 | 49.7 | 無數據 | 無數據 | 無數據 |
| 尼泊爾 | 46 | 39.2 | 44.5 | 54.1 |

把成千上萬顆的微粒集結在一起，都能裝進英文句子的句點裡。這樣的特性對人體極為有害，因為微粒可以深入你的肺部，而經常吸入過多的微粒，會導致許多嚴重的健康問題。

空氣汙染濃度的衡量單位是微克／立方公尺。每立方公尺 0 至 5 微克的濃度對人體健康的影響還好，但大多數國家的空汙濃度遠超過此數值，而且在某些空汙最嚴重的國家，其空汙濃度甚至超過安全值的十倍以上。下表列出了世界上空汙程度最嚴重的十個國家。這種表格裡的數字通常是按照行（橫向）、列（縱向）的方式編排，以便輕易查找所需的數字。

**35 台灣最厲害的殺手** P. 92

死亡讓人聞之色變，不過，了解一下死亡統計數據，能讓你為自身的健康擇善而行。台灣的衛生福利部每年都會公布上一年的死亡人數。2021 年，台灣的死亡人數就超過了 184,172 人，而造成死亡人數最多的疾病顯然就是癌症，奪走了 51,656 條生命。事實上，自 1980 年代以來，癌症就一直位居台灣的主要死因之冠。

請閱讀下頁的圓餅圖，圖中顯示了各種類型的癌症，以及 2021 年台灣罹患各類癌症的死亡人數。圓餅圖呈現的是各組成部分與整體之間的關係。整體是一個圓形，或稱之為「圓餅」（在本例中，圓形指的是台灣因癌症死亡的 51,656 人）；各組成部分則是圓餅圖的「扇形」。大家可從圖中得知，頭號的癌症殺手就是肺癌，而如今眾所皆知，造成肺癌的主因之一就是吸菸。因此，戒掉這種有害健康的惡習，就能減少成為罹癌統計數字一員的機率。

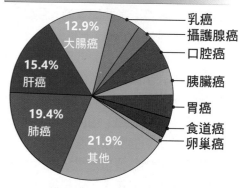

台灣各癌症死亡率（2021 年）

- 12.9% 大腸癌
- 15.4% 肝癌
- 19.4% 肺癌
- 21.9% 其他
- 乳癌
- 攝護腺癌
- 口腔癌
- 胰臟癌
- 胃癌
- 食道癌
- 卵巢癌

（來源：https://www.statista.com/）

## 3-2 參考資料

**36 女王的一生** P. 94

2022 年 9 月 8 日，全世界聽聞一件噩耗。英國女王伊莉莎白二世逝世，享耆壽 96 歲。她在位時間超過 70 年，成為史上統治時長排名第二的君主（譯註：有確切紀錄且獨立主權的君主）。她是一位深受歡迎的統治者，不僅受到英國臣民的愛戴，就連世界各地千百萬人也喜愛她。她逝世後，排隊想瞻仰她遺容的人龍綿延了 16 多公里！

以下是女王畢生重要事件的年表。年表是按照事件發生的先後順序列出。以此年表來說，事件是由左而右（從最早發生的一直到最晚發生的）依序列出。

## 女王伊莉莎白二世的一生

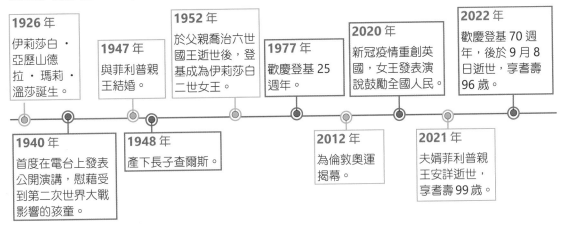

**1926 年**
伊莉莎白・亞歷山德拉・瑪莉・溫莎誕生。

**1940 年**
首度在電台上發表公開演講，慰藉受到第二次世界大戰影響的孩童。

**1947 年**
與菲利普親王結婚。

**1948 年**
產下長子查爾斯。

**1952 年**
於父親喬治六世國王逝世後，登基成為伊莉莎白二世女王。

**1977 年**
歡慶登基 25 週年。

**2012 年**
為倫敦奧運揭幕。

**2020 年**
新冠疫情重創英國，女王發表演說鼓勵全國人民。

**2021 年**
夫婿菲利普親王安詳逝世，享耆壽 99 歲。

**2022 年**
歡慶登基 70 週年，後於 9 月 8 日逝世，享耆壽 96 歲。

**37 研究心智** P. 96

人類的思維是如何運作的？我們為什麼會做出這樣的行為呢？這些都是心理學想解答的問題。

心理學是一門相當「年輕」的科學範疇，大約 150 年前才真正開始蓬勃發展起來。但是，我們當時仍大有斬獲，隨便在一家圖書館或書店的書架上，都能找到一排又一排心理學方面的書籍。不過，對剛入門的讀者而言，這類書籍讀起來可能晦澀難懂，就和別門科學一樣，心理學使用大量的專有名詞和學術用語，因此，閱讀心理學書籍時，手邊如果有術語表，就會很有幫助。

| A |
| --- |
| **成癮：** 無法停止做某事，尤其是對健康不利之事 |
| **青春期：** 人生中介於兒童到成人之間的一段時期 |
| **腎上腺素：** 人在感到興奮或害怕時，身體所釋放的一種化學物質，讓人的心跳加快 |
| **廣場畏懼症：** 害怕待在熱鬧的公共場所 |
| **利他主義：** 即使沒有報酬，也會關心他人的需求 |
| **失憶症：** 失去所有或部分的記憶 |
| **抗憂鬱藥物：** 用以減輕傷感情緒的藥物 |
| **焦慮：** 感到緊張或擔憂 |
| **失語症：** 失去使用語言的能力 |
| **自動化行為：** 不假思索做出的行為 |

術語表是一種精簡的字典，羅列了與特定主題相關的詞彙。跟字典一樣，這些詞彙同樣是按照 A 到 Z 的順序依序列出。下頁是心理學術語表的第一部分。

**38 時間控管！** P. 98

你常覺得自己時間不夠用嗎？也許你放學後想打個電動，但你花了太久的時間才把功課寫完；也許你想吃早餐，但你花了太久的時間才把書包整理好。如果這些事會發生在你身上，那麼你可能需要學著用更好的方式管理時間！

坊間有很多書在教大家怎麼做好時間管理，張蒂娜的著作《時間控管》就是一個例子，下頁列出該書的目錄。目錄會列出一本書裡的各個章節及其頁碼。瀏覽一下書籍的目錄，你就會對這本書的內容有更清楚的概念。

# 目錄

## 39　一起來玩園藝！　P. 100

　　你想要找個有趣又能感到充實的新嗜好嗎？何不試試園藝呢？照顧植物、看著它們生長，能讓人感到舒心，而且不需要寬廣土地，也能入門。如果你有一個陽台，甚至只是個窗台，任何陽光充足的地方，你就能玩園藝！你可以種種花、香草、蔬果等任何你喜歡的植物，隨心所欲主宰自己的花園！

　　如果你是園藝新手，參考新手指南是個不錯的做法。此類導引書籍會羅列出多種植物的資訊，還有幫助植物生長良好的小技巧和訣竅。如果想了解特定主題（例如「番茄」或「土壤」），只要翻閱後面的索引即可。索引會以 A 到 Z 的順序列出書中涵蓋的所有關鍵字，以及出現該關鍵字的頁數，因此能輕而易舉地查找特定資訊。

　　舉例來說，下頁提供了《園藝新手：園藝初體驗指南》一書的部分索引：

## 索引

## 40 哈囉，對自己笑一個吧！ P. 102

「自拍」，也就是用自己的手機給自己拍照，能帶來許多樂趣，但是有時很難拍出真正好看的照片。網路上有許多自拍方面的教學，教我們怎麼樣才能拍出好看的自拍照。想要找個教學內容來看，到網路上搜尋即可。當你在搜尋引擎上輸入一個字或語詞，然後再按下輸入鍵，網頁上就會列出一個個的網站，每個搜尋出來的網站都會有標題、網址和該網頁內容的簡短說明。以下就是輸入「自拍」後出現的搜尋結果。

www.what-words-mean.com/selfie

**「自拍」是什麼意思？——名詞解析**

「自拍」就是自己幫自己拍照的意思。大家通常是以手機或數位相機自拍……

www.tv-guide.org/shows/S/selfie

**自拍（電視劇）——電視節目表**

《自拍》是美國一齣喜劇片的片名，該劇於2014 年開播，由凱倫・吉蘭和趙約翰領銜主演……

www.culturemagazine.com/internet/may2014/how-selfies

**大家都在自拍，這是一件好事嗎？**
**——文化雜誌**

2014 年 5 月 12 日 瓊安・雪諾撰——從小孩到阿公阿嬤，如今人人都在自拍，但這新習慣是件好事還是件壞事呢？……

www.goodbuys.com.tw/phones/5TsTPN76

**自拍棒，一公尺長，非常堅固耐用，9.99 美元……**

一支一公尺長的自拍棒，以堅固的金屬材質製成，長度可伸縮，便於放入包包裡。現在購買只要 9.99 美元……

www.teenlife.net/blog/how-to-take-a-selfie

**如何自拍：拍出好看自拍照的八個訣竅**

2021 年 6 月 3 日——內容：1. 角度 2. 眼神
3. 光線 4. 笑容 5. 閃光燈 6. 取景
7. 找到自己好看的那一側 8. 練習。

# Unit 4 綜合練習

## 4-1 閱讀技巧複習

## 41 有型、實用又有趣 P. 106

在丹麥首都哥本哈根的市中心附近，出現了一座史上最令人驚艷的建築設計。這座名為「CopenHill」的建築是該市最高大宏偉的建築，但這並不是它別具一格的原因。CopenHill 建築的內外均不同凡響。

CopenHill 於 2019 年啟用，是全球最環保的垃圾焚燒發電廠，每年所焚燒的 44 萬噸垃圾，會轉換成足夠多的清潔能源，為當地十萬戶家庭供應電力與暖氣。而且，發電廠在轉換過程中並未將任何有毒物質釋放至大氣層。光是建築的內部就讓 CopenHill 舉足輕重，但更厲害的在後頭，這還是一座可供遊樂的建築。

CopenHill 的屋頂是個能讓大家享受戶外活動的場所，上面設有健行步道、遊樂場、健身區，還能俯瞰都市美景，而建築的外牆甚至可供攀爬。除了上述所有設施外，還有一條長達 450 公尺長的滑雪道，這是丹麥的第一條滑雪道。因此，CopenHill 不僅解決了垃圾的問題並供應能源，它還是一個重要的休閒娛樂場所。

CopenHill 是由比亞克 · 英格爾斯建築師事務所 BIG（譯註：Bjarke Ingels Group 的簡稱）所設計，這是一家由哥本哈根土生土長的建築師比亞克 · 英格爾斯所經營的公司。2011 年，該公司贏得一場競賽，拿到為哥本哈根市打造垃圾焚燒發電廠的建案，決定設計出一座功能更豐富的建築。如英格爾斯所說：「一座可永續發展的都市不僅更有利環保，亦能讓市民的生活更有樂趣。」

## 42 成為神祇的醫師 P. 108

你是否曾納悶，為什麼世界衛生組織的圖標是一條蛇盤繞在一根手杖上？蛇和手杖跟醫藥到底有何關係？事實上，這個符號與古希臘神話的醫療之神亞希彼斯有關。

相傳亞希彼斯是凡人女子科洛妮絲與太陽神阿波羅所生下的小孩。亞希彼斯小時候並未受到一般教育，他的父親送他到半人半馬的凱隆那裡撫養。凱隆以醫術聞名於世，他將自己一身的本領傳給了他的新學生。

亞希彼斯後來成為了一個很偉大的治療師，他也開始隨身攜帶一根盤繞著靈蛇的手杖，作為自己的象徵（因為希臘人認為蛇有特別的療癒能力）。然而，成也蕭何，敗也蕭何！由於他醫術精湛，以致於人們的壽命到了，卻都還健在。於是，冥神黑帝斯一狀告到眾神之王宙斯那裡。為了恢復世界的平衡，宙斯以一道閃電擊斃了亞希彼斯，此舉當然讓阿波羅大為震怒，為了求和，宙斯同意讓亞希彼斯也成為神祇。

古希臘時期，亞希彼斯的神殿成為了重要的醫療中心。人們會從四面八方遠道而來，到此尋求治療方法和研習醫術。如今，有許多人認為這些被稱為「Asclepieia」（俗稱「醫神廟」）的醫療中心是現代醫學的誕生地。

## 43 療癒身心的食物 P. 110

心情不好的時候，你會做什麼來讓自己好過一點呢？很多人會吃某些特定食物來舒緩心情，這類食物被稱為「療癒美食」。雖然每個人的療癒美食會因人而異，但一般而言，這類食物都有某些共同特質，通常熱量都很高，而且往往是零食（如洋芋片）或是偏油膩的家常料理（如奶油麵包布丁），口味通常偏甜或偏鹹，比較不會是酸酸的或苦苦的。不過，重點是，吃了這類療癒食物，會讓你由衷產生一種溫暖、開心的感覺。

那麼，這類食物何以會令人感到如此療癒？療癒美食通常會和快樂的回憶有關。特定食物（就像你奶奶做的巧克力蛋糕）之所以會讓你心情好，是因為它會讓我們想起所愛之人，以及與他們共度的快樂時光。此外，我們的身體喜愛高熱量的食物，因為它們能提供我們很多能量。我們吃下這些食物，大腦就會釋放出讓我們心情好的化學物質來獎勵我們。療癒美食十分強大，因為它們會影響我們的情緒和生理。

當然，偶爾吃吃你最愛的療癒美食沒有什麼不對。但由於療癒美食的熱量通常都很高，所以你每次心情不好就吃，可能不是什麼好主意。下次你想吃療癒美食的時候，請試著用別的辦法來改換心情，你可以去散散步或是悠哉地泡個澡。限制吃療癒美食的頻率，能防止這樣的習慣危及你的身體健康。

## 44 花園裡危機四伏 P. 112

大多數的人都喜歡坐在花團錦簇的花園裡。但請小心：我們身邊最常見的一些植物其實十分危險。

其中一種就是毒芹，這種看似無害的植物屬於蘿蔔科，但千萬別食用！它的莖充滿毒液，足以殺死人類和其他大型動物。大家可以從傘狀的白色小花輕易認出毒芹，不管在哪裡看到，都應該避開它。

再來是夾竹桃，在台灣和其他地方常栽種來作為造景花卉之用，其花卉有紅色、白色、粉紅色或黃色，看起來很可愛又易於照顧。不過，只要誤食一片葉子就會致命。諷刺的是，雖然夾竹桃會讓你的心臟永遠停止跳動，卻也被用來製作治療心臟病的藥物。

另一種需要留意的植物就是毒藤，雖然它的毒性不足以致死，但是觸碰到毒藤，會產生紅疹、搔癢和水泡的症狀。毒藤可生長至超過 30 公尺長。到戶外走動的時候，請以衣物遮蓋皮膚，保護自己免受毒藤的毒害。

杜鵑花屬的花卉是許多地方的熱門花種，包括台灣在內，於四、五月盛開，花色有紅色、紫色、白色、粉紅色、黃色、藍色以及上述花色的各種混色。然而，杜鵑花整株皆有毒性，會導致嘔吐、呼吸困難，甚至是昏迷。

簡單來說，當你身處上述這些植物的周遭時，觀賞就好，可千萬別去觸摸。

## 4-2 字彙學習複習

## 45 陪伴傾聽與協助 P. 114

首頁 > 學生服務 > 學生諮商

### 本校輔導老師可提供的協助

本校的輔導老師可協助學生處理各種問題，包括學業方面與個人生活方面的問題。我們的輔導老師會傾聽你的心聲並給予建議，他們不會批判你，只會幫助你。輔導老師可協助處理的事項如下：

- 考試壓力
- 被霸凌的問題
- 對國中生活感到緊張
- 家庭問題（如父母離異）
- 與某個班級或老師之間有矛盾
- 因壓力而想抽菸或吸毒

### 如何與輔導老師約談？

你可以隨時在輔導室開放的時間到輔導室來，預約與輔導老師的諮詢服務。別擔心預約的時間會和上課衝堂，輔導老師會告知你的老師你會缺席或晚到。

本校的輔導室位於 D 棟大樓四號會議室，開放時間為週一至週五上午八點至下午五點。

### 認識本校輔導老師

目前有三位輔導老師於橡木國中服務。請點選以下老師的姓名來了解更多相關資訊。

教師 波利・李 →　教師 詹姆斯・汗 →　教師 賽琳娜・拉米瑞茲 →

本校輔導老師均為輔導技能純熟的專業人員，有輔導年輕人的多年經驗。

**組裝說明書**

感謝您購買此桌（品項編號：23463566）。請仔細遵循以下步驟進行組裝。

**開始組裝前**

❶ 拆除木桌組件的塑膠包裝。

❷ 打開裝有五金零件的塑膠袋。

❸ 在開始組裝木桌前，請核對以下清單，確保所有零組件都有備齊。

❹ 如果零組件有缺件，請透過客服電話或到官網填寫表格與我們聯繫。

❺ 如果零組件無缺件，請將木桌組件置於乾淨的地面上，然後開始進行組裝。

**組裝步驟**

❶ 將桌面翻過來，桌面朝下放在地上。

❷ 將一支桌腳顛倒過來，倒扣在桌子的一角。

❸ 將桌腳上方的兩個孔洞和桌子一角的兩個孔洞對齊。

❹ 拿出一個墊圈，把一個螺栓穿過去，然後將帶有墊圈的螺栓旋入桌角的其中一個孔洞。（本說明書背面有圖示，清楚指示如何進行此步驟。）

❺ 使用 L 型六角扳手來旋緊螺栓。

❻ 以相同步驟處理第二個孔洞，此時桌腳應已牢牢穩固。

❼ 請重複步驟 2–6 來處理每一支桌腳。

❽ 最後將桌子擺正，置於想要放的位置。

| 五金零件 | | 數量 |
| --- | --- | --- |
| ⬡ | 墊圈 | 8 |
| 🔩 | 螺栓 | 8 |
| ⟍ | L 型六角扳手 | 1 |

| 木桌組件 | 數量 |
| --- | --- |
| 桌面 | 1 |
| 桌腳 | 4 |

　　當你犯錯的時候，會有什麼樣的舉止？你會罵自己很蠢，然後以鴕鳥心態逃避嗎？許多人會有這樣的反應，是因為他們將錯誤視為負面的事。然而，卻有很多因素可以讓我們將錯誤視為完全相反的意義。事實上，如果以正確的方式處理犯錯這件事，你就能體驗到許多收穫。

　　研究顯示，如果你犯了錯，但隨後思考自己哪裡做錯了，大腦中的神經細胞之間就會產生新的連結。犯錯其實能讓你的大腦增長！想要達到大腦增長的結果，你要學的不是去掩飾自己的過錯，而是去面對、去深刻思考這些錯誤。試著去想通自己哪裡做錯了，以後又能如何避免重蹈覆轍。

　　一旦你對自己承認「犯錯沒關係」，那扇通往許多新奇、令人心醉神迷的學習機會的大門都將為你敞開。沒有人一開始就是專家，但是日引月長，以及多次從錯誤中學習後，你就能成為專家。不知不覺間，你就已經多了一項技能。然而，如果你一直被犯錯的恐懼所束縛，你就會停滯不前，永遠不會有個人成長。切記，凡事皆可達成，只要你願意先犯錯！

　　「準時」到底是什麼意思？如果你遲到了五分鐘，還是算準時嗎？那麼十分鐘呢？一整天呢？「準時」的定義其實是因文化而異。以下是世界各地對準時定義的例子。

**墨西哥**  在墨西哥，遲到沒什麼大不了。以非正式的聚會或派對來說，晚到 30 分鐘幾乎是預料之中的事。

**日本** 在日本，遲到會被視作非常無禮的行為。事實上，大多數人都會儘量提前 10 到 15 分鐘抵達。如果你遲到了，最好做好道歉的準備！

**德國** 德國人非常看重準時這件事。遲到是沒有任何藉口的。塞車？那你就應該要事先規劃好，然後提早出門，不是嗎？

**摩洛哥** 摩洛哥人看待時間的態度是出了名的無所謂。在他們的標準裡，「準時」意味著從遲到 30 分鐘到一整天的時間！

**巴西** 此國家很習慣凡事延誤開始，如果在預定的時間現身在派對上，還會被視為無禮。為什麼？因為主人自己肯定會遲到，所以無法準備好來接待你！

## 4-3 影像圖表複習

**49 是毛還是羽毛？** P. 122

蝙蝠一度被認為是一種長相奇特的鳥類，但事實上，蝙蝠和鳥類是兩種迥異的動物。

蝙蝠是哺乳類動物，所以牠們屬胎生動物，會產下幼崽。蝙蝠的身體有毛覆蓋其身，有下顎和尖牙。牠們的飛翼其實是一雙很大的手，每隻手的指間有片皮膚薄膜相連。這片翼膜也將其前肢和後肢連接起來。由於蝙蝠在夜間覓食，偏偏牠們的視力又不佳，因此會用一種名為「回聲定位」的方法來找出獵物的位置。在捕食的過程中，蝙蝠會發出聲音，聲波碰到獵物會反彈回到蝙蝠身上，藉此得知獵物的位置。

鳥類不是哺乳類動物，牠們屬卵生動物，會產卵。鳥類渾身長滿羽毛，嘴巴有喙。鳥類也沒有手，只有一對堅實的翅膀。鳥類日夜皆可捕獵，但無論是什麼時段，牠們都是靠視力來尋找獵物。

當然，蝙蝠和鳥類確實有許多共同特徵。兩者都會飛，也都有能讓牠們飛行的流線型身形。此外，這兩種動物都是以昆蟲為食，而且都會照顧後代。

下方的文氏圖將鳥類和蝙蝠進行了比較。左圈裡描述了蝙蝠的特點，右圈裡描述了鳥類的特點，中間交集的部分則描述了蝙蝠和鳥類兩者間的共同點。

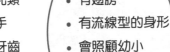

**蝙蝠**
- 以聲波捕獵
- 哺乳類
- 有手
- 有牙齒
- 有毛皮
- 胎生

（交集）
- 會飛
- 有翅膀
- 有流線型的身形
- 會照顧幼小
- 以昆蟲為食

**鳥類**
- 非哺乳類
- 沒有手
- 有喙
- 有羽毛
- 卵生
- 以視力捕獵

**50** **打造巧克力天堂的八個簡單步驟！** P. 124

　　巧克力慕斯是我最愛吃的其中一道甜點，它的口感滑順、濃郁，超級好吃。更重要的是，我什麼時候想吃都可以，因為這道甜點的製作方式非常簡單！所需的食材僅優質巧克力、蛋、牛奶、奶油和糖即可。經過幾個簡單的步驟後，我就能吃上一碗美味無比的巧克力慕斯！

　　以下是我用來製作這道美味甜點的食譜。食譜就是用一系列的步驟來教你如何做出一道餐點，也會告訴你製作這道餐點所需的食材為何，然後一步一步指導你食材的處理方式。

## 巧克力慕斯

**份量：2 人份**

**製作時間：10 分鐘（加上冷藏 2 小時）**

**所需食材：**

- 175 克的優質巧克力
- 1.5 大匙的牛奶
- 1.5 大匙的奶油
- 3 顆蛋
- 1.5 大匙的糖

**步驟 1：** 將巧克力切成小塊。

**步驟 2：** 把牛奶倒進小鍋子裡加熱。放入巧克力並攪拌直到融化，然後關火。

**步驟 3：** 融化奶油（可用微波爐），然後加到巧克力裡面。

**步驟 4：** 敲開蛋，分離蛋黃和蛋白，並分別放在不同的碗裡。

**步驟 5：** 將糖加在蛋黃裡混勻，再把蛋黃糖液加到巧克力裡拌勻。

**步驟 6：** 將蛋白打到乾性發泡，再倒入巧克力蛋黃糊裡，輕輕切拌。

**步驟 7：** 用勺子將幕斯糊挖到碗裡，然後放進冰箱冷藏2 小時即可。

**步驟 8：** 巧克力慕斯上桌，請盡情享用！

# Answer Key

## Unit 1　閱讀技巧

| 1 | 1.D | 2.B | 3.B | 4.C | 5.A | 11 | 1.D | 2.B | 3.C | 4.A | 5.C |
|---|-----|-----|-----|-----|-----|----|-----|-----|-----|-----|-----|
| 2 | 1.D | 2.D | 3.A | 4.C | 5.C | 12 | 1.B | 2.B | 3.D | 4.A | 5.D |
| 3 | 1.B | 2.D | 3.C | 4.A | 5.B | 13 | 1.D | 2.A | 3.C | 4.B | 5.A |
| 4 | 1.B | 2.A | 3.D | 4.D | 5.D | 14 | 1.D | 2.D | 3.B | 4.A | 5.B |
| 5 | 1.C | 2.C | 3.A | 4.C | 5.B | 15 | 1.C | 2.A | 3.D | 4.B | 5.D |
| 6 | 1.A | 2.B | 3.A | 4.B | 5.D | 16 | 1.D | 2.A | 3.C | 4.A | 5.B |
| 7 | 1.D | 2.B | 3.D | 4.B | 5.C | 17 | 1.C | 2.D | 3.D | 4.B | 5.A |
| 8 | 1.C | 2.A | 3.A | 4.C | 5.C | 18 | 1.D | 2.D | 3.B | 4.A | 5.C |
| 9 | 1.D | 2.D | 3.A | 4.C | 5.B | 19 | 1.A | 2.B | 3.C | 4.D | 5.B |
| 10 | 1.D | 2.C | 3.A | 4.C | 5.B | 20 | 1.C | 2.B | 3.B | 4.A | 5.C |

## Unit 2　字彙學習

| 21 | 1.D | 2.A | 3.C | 4.A | 5.B | 26 | 1.D | 2.C | 3.A | 4.C | 5.A |
|----|-----|-----|-----|-----|-----|----|-----|-----|-----|-----|-----|
| 22 | 1.B | 2.C | 3.A | 4.D | 5.B | 27 | 1.D | 2.C | 3.C | 4.A | 5.C |
| 23 | 1.B | 2.A | 3.C | 4.A | 5.C | 28 | 1.D | 2.D | 3.B | 4.A | 5.C |
| 24 | 1.B | 2.A | 3.C | 4.C | 5.A | 29 | 1.C | 2.A | 3.D | 4.C | 5.B |
| 25 | 1.B | 2.A | 3.C | 4.D | 5.A | 30 | 1.B | 2.A | 3.D | 4.B | 5.D |

## Unit 3　學習策略

| 31 | 1.A | 2.C | 3.A | 4.D | 5.D | 36 | 1.B | 2.D | 3.C | 4.A | 5.D |
|----|-----|-----|-----|-----|-----|----|-----|-----|-----|-----|-----|
| 32 | 1.C | 2.B | 3.C | 4.A | 5.D | 37 | 1.D | 2.D | 3.B | 4.B | 5.A |
| 33 | 1.D | 2.A | 3.C | 4.C | 5.A | 38 | 1.A | 2.A | 3.D | 4.A | 5.A |
| 34 | 1.D | 2.A | 3.C | 4.C | 5.B | 39 | 1.A | 2.B | 3.C | 4.D | 5.C |
| 35 | 1.B | 2.D | 3.A | 4.B | 5.D | 40 | 1.A | 2.B | 3.D | 4.D | 5.C |

## Unit 4　綜合練習

| 41 | 1.B | 2.D | 3.D | 4.A | 5.C | 46 | 1.B | 2.D | 3.C | 4.A | 5.C |
|----|-----|-----|-----|-----|-----|----|-----|-----|-----|-----|-----|
| 42 | 1.D | 2.C | 3.B | 4.A | 5.D | 47 | 1.D | 2.A | 3.B | 4.A | 5.C |
| 43 | 1.B | 2.D | 3.D | 4.C | 5.A | 48 | 1.A | 2.D | 3.C | 4.B | 5.D |
| 44 | 1.D | 2.B | 3.A | 4.B | 5.C | 49 | 1.B | 2.D | 3.C | 4.C | 5.A |
| 45 | 1.A | 2.D | 3.D | 4.B | 5.C | 50 | 1.C | 2.A | 3.D | 4.C | 5.B |

# 讀出英語核心素養 4

## 九大技巧打造閱讀力

| | |
|---|---|
| 作者 | Owain Mckimm |
| | Richard Luhrs（第 29 ／41 ／44 ／49 課） |
| | Laura Phelps（第 7 課） |
| | Shara Dupuis（第 6 課） |
| 譯者 | 劉嘉珮 |
| 審訂 | Helen Yeh |
| 企畫編輯 | 葉俞均 |
| 編輯 | 楊維芯 |
| 主編 | 丁宥暄 |
| 校對 | 黃詩韻 |
| 內頁設計 | 草禾豐視覺設計有限公司（鄭秀芳／顏玎如）／林書玉（中譯） |
| 封面設計 | 林書玉 |
| 圖片 | Shutterstock |
| 發行人 | 黃朝萍 |
| 製程管理 | 洪巧玲 |
| 出版者 | 寂天文化事業股份有限公司 |
| 電話 | 02-2365-9739 |
| 傳真 | 02-2365-9835 |
| 網址 | www.icosmos.com.tw |
| 讀者服務 | onlineservice@icosmos.com.tw |
| 出版日期 | 2022 年 12 月 初版一刷 |
| | （寂天雲隨身聽 APP 版） |
| 郵撥帳號 | 1998620-0 寂天文化事業股份有限公司 |

國家圖書館出版品預行編目 (CIP) 資料

讀出英語核心素養 . 4：九大技巧打造
閱讀力（寂天雲隨身聽 APP 版 )/Owain
Mckimm 著；劉嘉珮譯. -- 初版. -- [臺北市]
：寂天文化事業股份有限公司, 2022.12
　　面；　公分
ISBN 978-626-300-171-8( 平裝 )
1.CST: 英語 2.CST: 讀本
805.18　　　　　　　　111019276

訂書金額未滿 1000 元，請外加運費 100 元。

〔若有破損，請寄回更換，謝謝〕